PAINT
BY MURDER

KATE KINGSBURY

BERKLEY PRIME CRIME, NEW YORK

If you purchased this book without a cover, you should be aware that this book is stolen property. It was reported as "unsold and destroyed" to the publisher, and neither the author nor the publisher has received any payment for this "stripped book."

This is a work of fiction. Names, characters, places, and incidents either are the product of the author's imagination or are used fictitiously, and any resemblance to actual persons, living or dead, business establishments, events, or locales is entirely coincidental.

PAINT BY MURDER

A Berkley Prime Crime Book / published by arrangement with the author

PRINTING HISTORY
Berkley Prime Crime mass-market edition / September 2003

Copyright © 2003 by Doreen Roberts Hight.
Cover art by Dan Craig.
Cover design by Elaine Groh.

All rights reserved.
This book, or parts thereof, may not be reproduced in any form without permission.
The scanning, uploading, and distribution of this book via the Internet or via any other means without the permission of the publisher is illegal and punishable by law. Please purchase only authorized electronic editions, and do not participate in or encourage electronic piracy of copyrighted materials. Your support of the author's rights is appreciated.
For information address: The Berkley Publishing Group, a division of Penguin Group (USA) Inc., 375 Hudson Street, New York, New York 10014.

ISBN: 0-425-19215-6

Berkley Prime Crime Books are published by The Berkley Publishing Group, a division of Penguin Group (USA) Inc., 375 Hudson Street, New York, New York 10014.
The name BERKLEY PRIME CRIME and the BERKLEY PRIME CRIME design are trademarks belonging to Penguin Group (USA) Inc.

PRINTED IN THE UNITED STATES OF AMERICA

10 9 8 7 6 5 4 3 2 1

CHAPTER

1

Marlene Barnett clung to the handlebars of her bicycle and pedaled furiously along the coast road. She'd overslept that morning, and had woken up to the sound of rain peppering her bedroom window. By the time she'd gone downstairs, Polly had already left for the Manor House.

Now that her sister had wangled the job of assistant to Lady Elizabeth Hartleigh Compton, she left the house every morning at the crack of dawn. Ma thought it was because Polly was anxious to create a good impression. Marlene knew exactly why Polly broke her neck to get to work. It was so she could see Sam, her American boyfriend, before he left to go to the air base. Things weren't exactly rosy between Polly and her Sam, but at least they were still talking to each other.

Marlene gritted her teeth as the salty wind stung her face. If only she could be so lucky. The trouble with Yanks was they were fast workers. At least the good-looking ones were. One night out with them and they wanted to muck about. She should just forget the GIs. Find herself a limey instead. Yarmouth was full of British sailors looking for a good time.

Almost blinded by the wet wind, she didn't see the broken beer barrel until she was almost on it. Her violent wrench on the handlebars unbalanced her, and she squeezed the brakes, sending her back wheel into a skid on the wet road. She landed with a sickening bump in a puddle, with one foot entangled in the front wheel and brown mud streaked all over her raincoat.

Examining the ladder running up the front of her stocking, Marlene gave vent to a string of swear words that would have earned her boxed ears if Ma had heard them. She'd used up all her clothing coupons for that month. Now she'd either have to borrow some from Ma, or go around in laddered stockings.

As she struggled to free her foot, she heard a muffled roar in the distance. It sounded like something coming along the coast road. Vehicles from the American air base used the road sometimes, but this was no military Jeep or lorry. This sounded like a motorcar, and by the way the driver was revving the engine, he was in a big hurry.

Motorcars were not a common sight on the coast road, especially in wartime. People didn't go out for a drive anymore unless they were going somewhere, and that meant using the main road through the village to North Horsham. Or the London road. To have a car materialize right there at the exact moment she was sitting helplessly in its path struck Marlene as a cruel stroke of fate.

Frantically she tugged at her foot in a desperate attempt

to free it from her bicycle wheel. The sound intensified, and now she could see the vehicle looming through the mist of driving rain. She raised both arms, waved like mad, and yelled at the top of her voice.

For a terrifying moment she thought the metal monster might plow right over her. The tires squealed and slithered on the wet road, and she caught a glimpse of a white face behind the windscreen before the black bonnet swept past her and came to rest in the ditch at the side of the road.

Marlene's teeth chattered, and her entire body shook at her narrow escape. She watched anxiously as the door on the driver's side opened. A pair of long legs launched out onto the road, and the rest of a sturdy body followed. The man's head emerged, his face shadowed by the trilby he wore low on his forehead.

He came to her at a run, one hand gesturing wildly in the air, his harsh voice whipped by the wind. "What the bloody hell are you doing sitting in the middle of the road?"

Her fright dissolved in a hot flash of temper. "What the bloody hell do you think I'm doing? I fell off me bike, that's what. You almost ran me over. You could have killed me."

"Oh, Christ." He dropped to his knees beside her and pushed the brim of his hat back with his thumb. "Are you all right? Anything broken?"

"I don't think so. But my foot's caught in the wheel . . ." For the first time she got a good look at his face, and her words got lost with her breath. The scarf she'd tied around her head was dripping wet, her stockings were laddered, and her raincoat was covered in thick gooey mud. Trust her luck to meet the nicest-looking man she'd seen in ages when she was looking like she'd been working in the fields all day.

Then she remembered how he'd nearly killed her. "I can't get my foot out and I saw you coming and I was afraid—" To her embarrassment, her voice quivered and she snapped her mouth shut before she bawled.

"Oh, I say! Chin up, old girl." The man patted her awkwardly on the shoulder. "Let's see if I can get you free."

Impressed that he didn't seem to notice the knees of his nice trousers getting wet, Marlene allowed her resentment to cool. She winced when he grasped her ankle, then forgot her discomfort as his warm fingers manipulated her foot gently out of the bent spokes.

Shielding her eyes with her wet lashes, she studied him. Handsome bugger. Bit of a hooked nose, but otherwise he had soft brown eyes and a mouth that looked as if it smiled a lot.

The suit he wore must have set him back a bit, and his posh motorcar was bloody magnificent compared to the rusty old relics she usually saw in the High Street. By the way he talked, he didn't come from anywhere around Sitting Marsh, that she did know. This bloke was from the city. London, by the sound of it.

He chose that moment to look at her. Caught staring at him, Marlene felt her cheeks growing hot. She hastily switched her gaze to her foot. He still had hold of her ankle and she bent her knee to pull out of his grasp.

"How's it feel?" He wrinkled his brow at her. "Can you wriggle your toes?"

She nodded, flapping her foot up and down to show him. "It's all right, I think. Just a little sore."

The man scrambled to his feet and held out his hand. "Come on, then, ups-a-daisy. Let's see if you can stand on it."

Putting her hand in his, Marlene did her best to get to her feet without putting too much strain on him. It was one of the mysteries of life to her that while she and her sister ate the same amount of food, which wasn't that much now that everything was on ration, Polly was as skinny as a blade of grass and Marlene was what Ma called pleasantly plump. Which was just another way of saying she was fat. She was doing everything she could to correct that.

A sharp pain shot up her leg when she put her weight on it and she winced. "It's all right," she said bravely. "I can manage."

"I don't see how." Her companion picked up her bicycle and studied the mangled wheel. "I'm afraid this is going to take some straightening out."

Marlene engineered a helpless smile. "Well, it wasn't your fault. It was that beer barrel in the road. Must have fallen off the beer cart this morning." She looked down at her raincoat. "No wonder this mud is brown. It's probably beer stains. I'll never get it out."

"Beer barrel? Good Lord!" He stared at the wreckage in the road then spun around and thrust out his hand. "You probably saved my life. If I hadn't seen you sitting there waving at me, I would have smacked right into that mess. I'm in your debt . . . er . . . what is your name?"

Marlene grabbed the proffered hand and shook it. His grip was strong, and he seemed in no hurry to let her go. Fascinated by the gleam in his eyes, Marlene temporarily forgot her name. "Um . . . er . . . it's Marlene," she got out finally. "Marlene Barnett. I live in one of them cottages back there." She jerked a thumb over her shoulder.

"Very pleased to meet you, Marlene. I'm Peter Weston. Pete to my friends, actually."

Marlene reluctantly removed her hand from his grasp. "I'm sorry about your car. I hope it's all right."

"Oh, Lord, the jalopy. I'd better take a look."

She limped after him as he hurried over to the ditch. He leaned across the bonnet of the sleek sports car and she waited anxiously for his verdict.

After a moment or two he straightened and smiled at her. "Looks all right. Nothing a good body man can't straighten out. Hop in and start the engine and I'll try to shove it out."

Her eyes widened. "Me? I don't know nothing about driving a car."

"Oh, come on, old sport. Nothing to it." He tugged open the door. "Just get in and I'll show you what to do."

Nervously she slid onto the soft leather seat. It smelled like the new gloves Ma had given her for her birthday. Her hands shook when she placed them on the wheel.

Following Pete's directions she got the engine started. He showed her how to dip the clutch, slide the gears in reverse, then instructed her to hold her uninjured foot on the brake until he gave the signal.

She felt sick while she waited for him to climb down the ditch. What if she did it wrong? What if she went forward instead of backward and ran him over? Panic froze her fingers on the wheel. She saw his hand rise in a signal and all she could do was sit there, staring helplessly at him while the engine purred in expectation.

Pete gestured at her with an impatient flap. Closing her eyes, she took her foot off the brake and stepped on the accelerator. The engine roared, the car bucked, and Marlene screamed as she shot backward across the road heading straight for the cliff.

Dimly she heard Pete yelling something and instinct made her twist the wheel. Fortunately the sharp swerve swung her foot off the accelerator and onto the brake. With a series of lurches and bumps, the car came to rest at the very edge of the cliff. Marlene promptly lowered her head to the wheel and burst into tears.

The door flew open and a comforting male arm closed around her shaking shoulders. "Sorry, old sport. My fault. I should have told you just a light touch on the pedal."

Marlene lifted her face and glared at him through her tears. "I almost went over the cliff."

"I know." Pete wiped his forehead with the back of his hand, leaving a muddy streak beneath the dripping brim of his hat. "Scared the living daylights out of me, I can tell you."

"What the bloody hell do you think it did to me?" She snatched the wet scarf from her head and shook out her hair. "I nearly had a heart attack."

"Well, the least I can do now is drive you wherever you're going. We can chuck the bike in the back of the car. Shouldn't take much to get that wheel straightened. Your husband could do it."

"I'm not married."

"Boyfriend?"

He looked so hopeful she began to feel better. "No boyfriend, neither. At least not right now."

"Jolly good. Where do you want me to take you?"

"To the hairdresser's in the High Street, please. Next turning on the left."

"Right ho." He held out his hand. "Come on out then. You'll have to get in the other side. Unless you want to drive?"

His grin swept away the last of her apprehension. "Not on your life." She scrambled out and limped around to the passenger door. To her surprise, he followed her, opened the door for her, and helped her onto the seat. She didn't meet too many blokes with manners these days.

With a sigh of contentment, she leaned back to enjoy the ride.

"Hope you're not getting that gorgeous hair cut off," Pete said as he expertly shifted the gear lever. "I've always been fascinated by red hair."

Self-consciously, her hand brushed at the fringe hanging damply over her eyes. "It's not really red. More auburn. And I'm not getting it cut. I work at the hairdresser's."

He shot her a glance. "Oh, well, that's good. I can get you to cut my hair, then."

"I don't cut men's hair."

"Well, maybe I can change your mind about that. I'm going to be around for a while."

She couldn't help wondering why someone like him would want to stick around a dump like Sitting Marsh. She could tell he was no country bumpkin. What on earth could he find in her tiny village to keep him "around for a while"?

She thought about asking him, then decided it could wait. It was enough right now to anticipate the looks on everyone's faces when she sailed down the High Street in this posh car with a good-looking toff at her side.

"This is awfully good of you, Earl." Lady Elizabeth Hartleigh Compton clung to the wet rim of the Jeep as it careened around the sharp bend onto the coast road. One of the main complaints from the villagers about the Americans, and there were many, was that they drove too fast down the narrow English lanes. More often than not on the wrong side of the road.

Right then Elizabeth was inclined to agree, though she would die before she said so. Instead she flashed a smile at her handsome companion. "It would have taken me ages to walk to the cottages and it's such a beastly day."

Major Earl Monroe lowered his chin so that the peak of his cap protected his eyes. "I'm not sure this is any better. This Norfolk weather is something else. That wind cuts right to the bone."

"It's a nor'easter, as the fishermen call it. They can be quite ferocious at times." Elizabeth tugged her floppy yellow oilskin hat more firmly down on her head. She had to shout to be heard above the noise of the engine, and the wind took her breath away. She decided to wait until they arrived at Sandhill Lane before attempting any more conversation.

To her relief, the rain had stopped by the time they reached the cottage at the end of the lane. The silence when Earl shut off the engine was blissful. "Well," she said breathlessly, "it's true what they say about the English seaside. If the weather isn't to your liking—"

"Just wait five minutes," Earl finished for her. "I think it was one of our guys who said it first." He eyed her with a look of concern on his rugged face. "You look a mess."

"Thank you. You're so kind." Elizabeth carefully removed the offending hat, sending a spray of raindrops into her lap. "It's awfully difficult to look elegant when traveling a hundred miles an hour in the teeth of a nor'easter. But one must make the best of it, I suppose."

Earl grinned. "We were barely doing thirty. I've seen you go faster than that on your motorbike."

She chose to ignore that. "Well, thank you anyway. This was much faster than walking."

"You bet it was. When did you say your bike will be ready?"

"I didn't." Elizabeth stuck a hairpin more firmly into her French twist, which right now seemed in danger of unwinding. "But I imagine it will be ready by the time I walk into the town this morning. After I've talked to Mr. Thorncroft, that is. I really feel quite guilty about not welcoming him before this. He rented the cottage three weeks ago. I should have come down earlier."

Earl shook his head. "I can never figure out why you chase all over the countryside on that darn motorbike in weather like this just to pay a visit to your tenants. Doesn't fit the image of a lady of the manor somehow."

Not sure if she should be offended by his comment, Elizabeth frowned at him. "Oh? What would you say the image should be? Sitting meekly in the parlor entertaining the gentry while we all sip tea?"

He shrugged. "Something like that, I guess."

"How utterly boring." Elizabeth watched his tall figure stride around the bonnet of the jeep, marveling as usual at his ability to appear light on his feet despite his sturdy build. "The most interesting part of being guardian of this estate is getting to know the villagers. How else am I going to know how best to serve them if I don't know their problems and concerns?"

Earl held out his hand and helped her down from the Jeep. "I reckon there's enough people in the village who'd let you know soon enough."

"You're right about that. But the Hartleighs have always been highly accessible to the people and it's especially important now that we have this dreadful war. The villagers need to know that someone is in control, and watching out for them. Remember, when my father died, they lost the last Lord Wellsborough in a long line of earls dating back more than two hundred years. It's been difficult for them to accept a woman in their place, and the only way I can gain their trust is to be among them as often as possible. But then you know all that. I've explained it all to you often enough."

"I guess so . . . I just worry about you, that's all."

The little thrill she always felt when he said something nice made her smile. "Well, I'm a lot sturdier than I appear. To be honest, I rather enjoy sailing up and down the hills on my motorcycle." A gust of wind tugged at her scarf and she tucked it firmly into the neck of her coat. "Though I must admit, on days like this one I wouldn't mind having a motorcar to ride in. Not that I know how to drive one." She looked up in surprise as Earl grasped her arm and began walking with her to the gate of the cottage. "Aren't you going to the base?"

"Later. There won't be any missions in this weather, so I have time to take you into town to pick up your motorbike."

She started to protest, but he silenced her with an uplifted hand. "No arguments, okay?"

Any argument would have been halfhearted on her part anyway, she thought happily as she waited for him to open the garden gate.

Their feet crunched on the wet pebbles lining the path that led up to the small porch. Earl paused as they reached the steps. "Maybe I should wait outside."

"Nonsense. You were kind enough to give me a lift down here, and I'm certainly not going to leave you out here in the cold wind." Elizabeth stepped up to the front door and lifted the brass knocker. Letting it fall, she added, "I'm sure Mr. Thorncroft will be happy to see visitors. I understand he doesn't get out much. He's an artist, you know."

Earl seemed unimpressed. "What kind of artist?"

Elizabeth lifted her shoulders. "Oh, I don't know. Seascapes, I suppose. Violet says she's seen him sitting on the cliffs with his easel and paints."

"Not in this weather, I bet."

"Which is why I chose to come down this morning." She frowned, and peered into the side window of the front room. "Though it does appear that he's not home after all."

"Perhaps he didn't hear you." Earl lifted the knocker again and rapped hard. As he did so, the door uttered a loud squeak and swung open.

"Oh, dear. He must have forgotten to latch the door." She leaned forward. "Are you there, Mr. Thorncroft? It's Lady Elizabeth. I just wanted to welcome you to the village."

After a moment or two of silence, Earl said quietly, "Guess he's out there painting after all."

"In the rain?" Elizabeth shook her head. "He's more than likely gone into town. I'll just make sure this door is properly latched. In this wind it could blow—" She broke off abruptly as something in the front room caught her eye—a rumpled pile of clothes on the floor in front of the large tweed couch.

"Oh, good heavens!" Without waiting for Earl, she plunged into the room. As she'd suspected, it wasn't a pile of clothes at all. Basil Thorncroft lay on the floor, and judging by the ugly dark red stain soaking the front of his yellow silk shirt, he wasn't getting up anytime soon.

CHAPTER

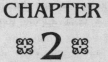 2

"All right, ladies! Pick up those feet and march. One, two, one, two . . ." Rita Crumm's shrill voice defied the wind as she strode in front of a straggly line of women along the coast road like an impatient stork leading its youngsters home.

"I wish she'd put a sock in it," a buxom housewife muttered. "It's too blinking early to be out here in this weather. If the Germans landed now, none of us would have the bleeding strength to bash 'em over the head."

"Here, Marge, don't you let our Rita hear you say that." Her companion nudged her arm. "She'll have us parading around the square half the afternoon. Worse than a blinking sergeant major, she is."

"You're telling me." Marge puffed harder as she tried

to keep up with the rest of the group. "Anyone would think she's trying to win the war all by herself."

Clara chuckled. "Of course she is. Didn't you know that?"

"Halt!" The order screeched down the line. "Stop that nattering back there. How do you expect to have enough breath to march if you're chattering like magpies all the time?" Rita stuck her fists into her hips and glared at her motley followers. "Now gather 'round. I have some orders to give you and I want to be sure everyone hears them in this wind."

Rita Crumm's bony body made her appear fragile, but her will was indomitable and her voice could carry all the way to North Horsham—wind or no wind.

"Why do we have to come out in the rain?" someone whined in the back of group.

"Because the Germans are not going to let a bit of rain stop them, are they?" Rita waved an arm at the boiling ocean. "This is the kind of day they'd choose to invade us. When we least expect it. We have to patrol this road day and night if we're going to stop them from surprising us."

"They're the ones what'll get the surprise if they try to cross the North Sea in that wind," someone suggested.

"I can't see us stopping them anyhow when they've got bayonets and rifles and all we've got is a bunch of sauce-pans."

This comment was answered by a chorus of agreement from the group.

At the end of her patience, Rita's temper exploded. "I keep telling you until I'm bloody blue in the face. We're not going to fight them off. We'll catch them in the act of landing and we'll ring the church bells to alert the village."

"Yeah, then the rest of them can fight the Germans off with saucepans."

"No, with bedpans," someone answered. "The stink will turn them back into the sea."

A frail-looking woman laughed nervously and earned a ferocious glare from Rita. "Listen to me, you measly bunch of ninnies," she yelled. "If we don't do our job out here, them Nazis could sneak in behind our backs and we'd never know they were here. I'm not just talking about soldiers with guns. I'm talking about spies as well."

A babel of chatter broke out among the group.

"Spies?"

"Bloody hell."

"What do spies do?"

"Spy on you, that's what."

"What for?"

"What would a spy be doing here in Sitting Marsh?"

Rita drew breath for another tirade. "Spies learn secrets about us and tell the enemy, you nitwits. I heard that there could be one here in the village. That's why we have to keep our traps shut about the war. Anyone could be a spy. Your next door neighbor could even be a spy."

Marge looked dumbfounded. "Crikey! Old Mother Barker could be a blinking spy?"

A shout of laughter answered her.

"Yeah," Clare muttered. "She keeps her secrets in them red bloomers she wears."

"They're certainly big enough," Nellie Smith chimed in. "I've seen them hanging on the line. Make really good sails for a yacht, they would."

"Quiet!" Rita's roar finally penetrated the group. "Get into a proper line. At least try to look as if you're members of the Housewives League instead of a bunch of Brownies on a picnic."

"What about that man over there?" Florrie Evans piped up. "He could be a German spy."

Everyone stopped muttering and stared in the direction indicated by Florrie's shaking finger.

Rita puffed out her irritation at being interrupted again. Slowly she turned, ready to dismiss the target of their interest and deliver a scathing comment on the ignorance of her hapless followers. Instead, she paused, narrowing her eyes.

The man stood near the edge of the cliff with his back to the group of women, apparently unaware of their existence. As he turned his head this way and that, Rita could see quite clearly that he held a pair of binoculars to his eyes.

Excitement gripped her as she stared at him, her mind racing with indecision. He certainly was a stranger. What if he really *was* a spy? Should her Housewives League tackle the man? After all, he was heavily outnumbered. But what if he had a gun? Then again, he could hardly shoot them all before they were on him.

Rita was fairly confident that should the occasion arise and the order given, her makeshift army would charge to the forefront, thus shielding her from a possible bullet. On the other hand, someone would undoubtedly be hit, and much as she longed to destroy the enemy, she didn't want the death of one of her ladies on her conscience.

The women behind her had grown silent, each anxiously waiting for their stalwart leader's decision. Reluctantly abandoning her visions of glory, Rita turned back to her apprehensive crew. "I suppose we should find out what he's doing up here. We'll walk past him, as if we're out on a morning stroll. No one say anything, all right? Let me do the talking."

"If you ask me, you can do the walking past him as well," Marge muttered darkly.

"Why don't we just stroll back the way we came?" Nellie's suggestion raised a smattering of agreement from the group, much to Rita's disgust.

"Stroll back the way we came? What's the matter with you lot? I thought we all agreed when we formed this league that we would do whatever we could to protect Sitting Marsh from the enemy. Even if it meant laying down our lives."

"I don't remember promising to lay down anything," Margo protested.

"It was in the oath," Clara reminded her.

"If I'd realized that, I wouldn't have blinking sworn it."

"Be quiet!" Rita's glare swept the entire entourage. "Now, everyone look casual and follow me. Remember, let me do all the talking." Squaring her shoulders, she led the group toward the lone figure on the cliffs.

She was a few yards away when the man apparently caught sight of her. He hastily lowered his binoculars and tucked them inside his raincoat, leaving a huge bulge that made his chest look deformed.

Noting the furtive movement, Rita tried to look pleasant as she nodded at him, though her heart thumped madly against her ribs. "Morning!" she called out "Nice day for a stroll. Isn't it?"

The rain had plastered the man's dark hair to his head. His small, beady eyes seemed set too close together above a long, pointy nose, reminding Rita of a rat.

"The ladies and I like to take a walk along this road every morning. Isn't that right, ladies?" she went on, beginning to panic under the hard scrutiny of the mysterious stranger. "We never miss, not once. It's good for the lungs." She hesitated, then daringly added, "Can't say we've seen you here before."

Instead of answering her, the man turned his gaze to a spot farther down the road. Fearing he had an accomplice, Rita spun around, and nearly choked. No wonder the bloke was looking at her as if she was crazy. Instead of casually strolling along behind her, her brave group of warriors had stayed right where she'd left them, huddled together and clinging to each other in a way that left no doubt of their alarm.

Cursing under her breath, Rita turned back to the man. "They don't like strangers," she said hopefully.

"Obviously." He gave her another of his intense stares.

Desperate now, Rita nodded her head up and down. "Enjoying the view, are we?" She waited for his answer, wondering how fast she could run back to the others if he decided to attack her.

After a long pause, he said with obvious reluctance, "I happen to be a bird-watcher. I'm studying the migration of various species from the marshes."

His precise accent helped to steady Rita's nerves a little, though a small voice reminded her that German spies usually spoke perfect English. "A bird-watcher! How interesting!" Her suspicions only partly allayed, she added casually, "Isn't it awfully hard to see them in the rain?"

His lips visibly tightened. "I don't have a lot of time. I have to be back in London by next week." He glanced at the group of women now advancing at a snail's pace. "Well, don't let me keep you from your . . . stroll." His hesitation on the last word was accompanied by a sardonic glance at the stormy sky.

Rita took one last shot. "We have a pretty good bird-watching society in Sitting Marsh. I'm sure they'd be happy to share what information they have. I do believe they have a meeting this week. Where shall I tell them to get ahold of you?"

For a moment she thought he wasn't going to answer. Then, with a quick look at the advancing women, he muttered, "You can find me at the Tudor Arms." With that, he took off down the road, the hem of his soggy raincoat flapping around his legs.

She called out after him. "You didn't tell me your name!"

He either didn't hear her, or didn't want to answer her. He just kept going, his head bent against the wind, his arms pumping at his sides.

"What'd he say, what'd he say?" demanded a chorus of voices behind her.

Rita spun around. "Fat load of bloody good you lot are." She waved her arm at the retreating man. "What if he'd been a spy? He could have chucked me over the cliff."

"We told you to go back the way we'd come," Florrie reminded her through chattering teeth.

"Wars don't get won by retreating." Rita tugged her red woolly hat more firmly onto her head. Now that the apparent danger was over, her confidence was fast returning. "Anyway, he said he was a bird-watcher. Staying at the Tudor Arms." Although she didn't say so out loud, something about the man disturbed her. It wouldn't hurt to have a word with the constables, she decided. Let them take care of it. She'd had quite enough adventure for one day. "Come on," she said, starting off down the road, "let's get warmed up with a cup of tea at Bessie's."

"So, why would a pretty girl like you bury herself in a tiny village like this?" Pete Weston asked as the car sped down the hill toward town.

Marlene fluffed her hair with her fingernails and smiled. "I like living in Sitting Marsh. It's better than being blown to bits by a bomb in London."

"Well, yes, I have to give you that."

Her curiosity finally got the better of her. "Is that where you come from? London?"

"Surrey, actually. I suppose the American air force chaps help to liven things up a bit, don't they?"

Marlene shrugged. "I s'pose so. I'm getting a bit tired of all the fuss about them, to be honest."

"Why? Don't you like them?"

"Most of them are all right. Some of them are just looking for a good time. A girl could get herself in trouble if she didn't watch out."

"But not you, though, I bet."

She sent him a sidelong glance, wondering what he was getting at. "Of course not. I've been brought up respectable. My ma would kill me if I took that kind of trouble home."

"What about your friends? Do they spend much time with the Americans?"

"Some of them." She hesitated, then decided there was no harm in telling him about Polly. "My sister is sweet on a Yank, actually. He's an officer billeted up at the Manor House. Been going together some time they have. Though things aren't too good with them right now. See, Sam had an accident and his face got all bashed up, and now he won't have nothing to do with our Polly. She's not giving up on him, though."

"The Manor House? Where's that?"

A little miffed at his apparent lack of interest in her younger sister's romance, Marlene jerked a thumb over her shoulder. "It's back there on the hill. Great big house, it is. You must have seen it when you came down the coast road."

"Oh, right. The mansion. I did see it. So, your sister works there?"

"Yeah, she's Lady Elizabeth's secretary."

"Fancy that. Is there a lord living there, too?"

"Not anymore. See, Lord and Lady Wellsborough were killed in an air raid in London and Lady Elizabeth had to take over because there weren't no sons and no earl anymore."

Pete nodded his head. "I see. It's a big house. Who else lives there?"

"Just Lady Elizabeth; Martin, the butler; and Violet, the housekeeper. Oh, and Sadie Buttons. She's the housemaid. Then there's the Yanks."

"Ah, then there's more than one American living at the Manor?"

"Yeah, there's about a dozen of them." Marlene squirmed in her seat. His questions were beginning to make her uncomfortable. She decided to ask a few of her own. "So what are you doing in Sitting Marsh? It's a bit late in the year to be on holiday."

"Just looking around. How far is the American base from here? Do the G.Is come into the village very often?"

"Often enough." She stared at him, trying hard to read his expression. "Why are you so interested in the Yanks?"

He shot her a quick glance, then looked back at the road. "Actually, I'm more interested in you. How about showing me around this great town of Sitting Marsh when you get off work today?"

"I'm busy tonight." She'd spoken without thinking, put off by his probing questions. Relieved to see they were approaching the High Street, she pointed at the windscreen. "My shop is just up there on the right. See the sign outside?"

He leaned forward, his eyes narrowed. "The Country Boutique. Sounds impressive."

"We do all right." She grabbed the door handle as he slid to a stop in front of the hairdresser's. "Thanks ever so much for the lift."

He twisted in his seat to face her. "Marlene, I'd really like to take you out tonight. Anywhere you want to go. It's the least I can do after giving you such a fright this morning. I swear I'll be a perfect gentleman."

She wavered. Out of the corner of her eye she could see a couple of girls in the shop gazing openmouthed at her through the window. A small group of housewives waiting in a queue at the butcher's shop were all staring in her direction as if they'd never seen a posh car before. She rather liked being the center of attention. What would Polly and Ma say if a car like this pulled up outside their little cottage to pick her up? Ma would have a fit. Polly would be really jealous.

It was this last thought that made up her mind. Although Marlene would never admit it, she envied Polly's romance with Sam. They'd been going strong for months now . . . at least they had until the accident. Even now, with Sam keeping out of her way, Polly was determined they'd get back together again. Sam was her whole world, and nothing mattered to her more than being with him.

Marlene wanted very badly to feel that kind of passion about someone. After all, she was three years older than Polly. It wasn't fair. It would be nice if Polly envied her for once.

"All right," she said quickly, before she could change her mind again. "You can take me to the pictures in North

Horsham. It's not too far from here. There's a film with Ronald Coleman I'd like to see."

"I'll be at your house at seven o'clock. What number is it?"

His smile washed away all her lingering doubts. He did have awfully kind eyes. And dressed really nice. She'd never been out with a toff before. It would be fun to make the people in this town sit up and take notice.

She told him the number of her house, her mind already envisioning what she could wear.

"Right. I'll see you tonight then. Hold on a minute."

Mystified, she watched him climb out of the car and hurry around the bonnet to her side. When she realized he was opening the door for her, she couldn't help sending a smirk of satisfaction in the direction of the hairdresser's window.

Her grand moment was marred somewhat when she caught her heel in the doorway and almost dived headfirst to the pavement, but it was worth the slight embarrassment when Pete grabbed her arms to steady her and she saw the girls nudging each other.

Playing it for all she was worth, she gazed up at him with her best imitation of Veronica Lake, her favorite film star. "I'll see you tonight then," she said, trying to make her voice husky.

For an unsettling moment she thought he was going to kiss her, but then he let go of her and touched the brim of his hat in a brief salute. "I'm looking forward to it."

She watched him stride around the car and climb in. Then, with a wave, he roared up the High Street and out of sight. Smiling to herself, Marlene marched into the hairdresser's, where she was met with a bombardment of eager questions.

It was only then that she realized she knew very little

about Peter Weston, yet he knew a whole lot about her. The thought bothered her, but she brushed it aside as she basked in the avid interest of the women in the shop. There'd be time enough to find out more about the good-looking stranger. She had the whole evening ahead to get to know him—and she was looking forward to it more than anything in a long time.

CHAPTER

❀ 3 ❀

"Well, you can forget about renting that cottage again." Violet pounded the slab of pastry dough on the kitchen table with her rolling pin, sending a puff of white dust in the air. The front of her pinafore was coated with flour, as was the side of her scrawny cheek.

Seated on the other side of the table, Elizabeth surveyed her housekeeper with a wary eye. She was dying for a cup of tea, but knew better than to interrupt Violet's schedule.

Violet and Martin were the only ones left out of a household of servants who had long ago abandoned servitude in favor of more lucrative pursuits. Although she was technically an employee, the housekeeper's long

25

years of service entitled her to a place in the household
more or less as a family member.

Having lost both her parents in a bombing raid on London, Elizabeth was deeply grateful for Violet's loyalty and
affection, and overlooked the fact that the woman at times
forgot her place and acted more like a mother than a
housekeeper. Though right now, she was a little put out
by Violet's assumption.

"I don't see why I should have trouble renting the cottage. Once it's cleaned up, of course. There was very little
blood on the carpet, all things considered. It shouldn't be
a problem at all."

"Well, all I'm saying is, that someone might not be so
quick to rent it when they find out that two people died
in that cottage. Bad luck, that's what it is." Violet picked
up the square of dough by two corners, slapped it upside
down, and began rolling it again.

Elizabeth pursed her lips. "The cottage is almost two
hundred years old. It would be very surprising if no one
else had died there in all that time."

"You know what I mean. What with that Fred Bickham
dying in his bed, and now this poor bugger. You almost
died in there yourself, once. There's something evil about
that cottage. You mark my words."

"Fred Bickham died of a heart attack," Elizabeth said
firmly.

"Well, this artist bloke certainly didn't, did he." Violet
reached for a pie plate and draped the dough over it.
"Someone blinking did him in, didn't they."

"It certainly seems like it. The poor man was apparently
stabbed through the heart. I can't imagine why someone
would want to kill Mr. Thorncroft. He seemed such a
quiet, harmless man, though he was rather withdrawn. I
got the impression he didn't like to talk about himself.

All he'd tell me was that he'd moved down to the seaside to paint full time, and that he used to work in London repairing bomb damage to houses."

"Well, not everyone likes to air their dirty linen. There must have been something wrong in his life for him to get murdered like that."

Elizabeth sighed. "I suppose you're right, since it doesn't seem to be a robbery. Though I can't think the culprit could be anyone local. Mr. Thorncroft hadn't been here long enough to get to know anyone. From what I hear, he wasn't too outgoing."

"Most of them artist types aren't." Violet deftly trimmed around the plate and gathered the pieces of dough together. "You think someone followed him down from London to do him in?"

"I don't know what to think."

"Well, the constables will have fun with that one. After all, George and Sid are not exactly experts on murder investigations. I'll never understand what possessed Scotland Yard to bring them out of retirement like that. For all the good they are, they could have recruited a couple of farm lads."

"They didn't have much choice, with all our able-bodied men called up for military duty." Elizabeth sighed. "I'm afraid I have to agree with you, though. By the time our constabulary have finished trampling around the cottage, it's unlikely there'll be any clues left to tell us who killed the poor man."

Violet tilted her head to one side. "I take it they wouldn't let you help them look for clues."

"Of course not." Elizabeth reached across the table and removed a slice of apple from the large bowl at Violet's elbow. "Though I did take a look around while Earl went down to the police station to fetch George."

"Did you find anything?"

"I couldn't see anything that was out of place. The poor man must have been taken by surprise." Elizabeth munched on her apple. "There were paintings stacked against all the walls, and a lovely seascape sitting on the easel in the parlor. A truly beautiful sunset. It would have looked marvelous hanging on the wall in my office."

"So what's going to happen to the cottage now?"

"Well, it's off limits for a day or two, while George and Sid conduct their investigation. They'll contact Mr. Thorncroft's aunt—I believe she's the only relative the unfortunate man had—and once his belongings have been taken care of, we can clean up the cottage and see about renting it again."

"Good luck," Violet muttered. "I must say, I don't feel very comfortable with a murderer running around Sitting Marsh. I hope those two fools at the police station find the bloke who did it before he stabs someone else in the heart." She lifted the bowl and tipped the apple slices onto the pastry. "As if we don't have enough to worry about, what with the Germans about to invade us and Yanks causing all that trouble in the village, not to mention the lot we've got billeted here."

Elizabeth lifted her chin. "It's not only Americans who cause trouble in the village. The British soldiers, not to mention the few men left in the village, must share the blame for that. If they'd just learn to get along with each other—"

"They're never going to get along with each other as long as them Yanks are turning the heads of all the women. Even you're not exactly immune to their fancy talk."

Elizabeth felt her cheek begin to burn. There were some areas where even Violet was forbidden to tread. "If you're talking about Major Monroe, he is a guest in our house. He treats me with the utmost respect. I shouldn't have to remind you again that he has a wife and family waiting for him in America."

Violet rolled out the ball of dough and began cutting it into wide strips. "Maybe you should remind yourself of that now and again."

"I beg your pardon?"

She laid down the rolling pin. "I just don't want to see you hurt again, Lizzie. After that rotten ex-husband of yours gambled away every penny you had, I should think you'd be more careful with your affections."

Elizabeth rose to her feet. "Not that it's any of your business, Violet, but as I've told you many times before, the major and I are friends. Nothing more."

Violet's lips thinned. "I wouldn't be too sure of that if I were you."

Elizabeth was about to ask what she meant by that when the door opened abruptly behind her. Two boisterous dogs joyfully chased each other into the kitchen, followed by the hunched figure of Martin.

As usual he was nattily dressed in striped trousers and a dark coat over a maroon velvet waistcoat. The top button of the waistcoat was undone, she noticed, and something else seemed different, though she couldn't make out what that was right at that moment.

Martin bowed when he saw her. "Good day, madam. I failed to see you return this morning. I trust the horses have been taken to the stables? I can't seem to remember having seen Willis about lately. I do hope he hasn't gone off somewhere and left us in the lurch again."

Elizabeth exchanged a resigned glance with Violet. Martin's encroaching senility was a source of constant concern for both of them. Although Elizabeth was determined to ignore her butler's inability to properly fill his duties, even to the extent of taking care of them herself at times, she couldn't help worrying about the frail, elderly man who had been such a prominent member of the household for more than sixty years.

"Willis is no longer with us, Martin," she reminded him gently.

He looked startled. "Good Lord! Then who's taking care of the horses, may I ask?"

Violet, who possessed none of Elizabeth's patience, said crisply, "There aren't no flipping horses, Martin, so stop fussing about them."

"No horses?" Martin ran a trembling hand over the few gray hairs he had left. "What happened to them?"

"They got replaced by bicycles." Violet sent a disapproving look in Elizabeth's direction. "Some of them with motors in them, which were never meant for ladies to ride."

Determined not to be drawn into an old argument, Elizabeth patted Martin's arm. "Sit down, Martin. Violet was about to make us a nice cup of tea, weren't you, Violet."

She looked hopefully at the housekeeper, who shrugged and reached for the kettle.

Martin hovered over the empty chair at the table. "May I have your permission to join you at the table, madam?"

"You may, Martin."

"Thank you, madam."

"Not at all." Elizabeth smiled fondly at him.

Martin took his time getting seated, while Violet filled the kettle and sat it on the stove. Once settled, he lowered his chin to peer across the room over the top of gold-rimmed glasses. "If you don't mind my asking, madam, could you please tell me the time? My eyesight isn't what it used to be."

Violet tutted under her breath. "You could see perfectly well, you silly old fool, if you'd look through your glasses instead of over them."

Martin transferred his gaze to frown at the housekeeper. "I wasn't aware I was addressing you, Violet, so kindly keep your useless opinions to yourself."

"It's almost noon," Elizabeth said, in an effort to stave off the inevitable argument. "We'll be having lunch before too long."

"That's all he does nowadays," Violet muttered. "Eat, sleep, and get underfoot. Worse than Gracie and George, he is."

Elizabeth smiled fondly at the chubby dogs, who were rolling over each other on the rug in front of the stove. Earl Monroe had presented her with the puppies, and named them after characters in a American radio show. "I wonder what our constable, George, would say if he knew he shared his name with a dog."

"Don't know why he should mind, considering they both have the same amount of intelligence," Violet muttered.

Elizabeth didn't answer her. Something else had occurred to her, and she stared at Martin, who seemed absorbed in the effort to fasten the top button of his waistcoat. She knew now what was missing—the gold chain that usually looped from his pocket. "Martin? Where is your pocket watch?"

Martin avoided her gaze. "I'm not sure, madam. I seem to have misplaced it."

Violet spun around from the stove. "You lost your watch? Martin, how could you have lost it? The master gave you that for fifty years of service. It's worth a small fortune."

Martin lifted his chin. "I know how much it's worth. I

didn't intentionally misplace it. I put it down somewhere, and at this particular moment I can't remember where that is."

Violet's eyes rolled upward. "You'd forget your head if it wasn't screwed on."

"Well, ask Sadie to look for it." Elizabeth rose to her feet.

Violet frowned at her. "Going somewhere?"

"I want to stop by the police station. If we're to get the cottage cleaned and ready for a new tenant, I need to know when we can get in there." She paused at the door. "I'm hoping Sadie can go down there tomorrow. We can't afford to let it sit empty for long."

"Why don't you just have Polly call them." Violet glanced at the clock on the mantelpiece. "It'll be lunchtime soon."

"I won't be long." Elizabeth closed the door between them before Violet could argue. She wasn't about to admit to her housekeeper that she had more than one reason to visit the police station. A tenant of hers had been brutally murdered. The man who did it was still at large, possibly still in Sitting Marsh.

As guardian and chief advisor for the estate and its tenants, it was her duty to make sure that everything was being done to apprehend the criminal. Knowing the constables as well as she did, they might just need a shot in the arm. And she was just the person to give it to them.

When she arrived at the police station later, she found the front office empty. Judging by the sound of raised voices erupting from the back room, George and Sid were engaged in one of their usual arguments. She had to pound the bell on the desk quite severely for several seconds before the voices cut off, and a loud scraping sound suggested that at least one of the men had left his seat.

George's voice sounded impatient as he appeared in the doorway. "All right, all right, hold your bleeding horses—" The last word was hastily covered by a grating cough when he caught sight of his visitor. "Lady Elizabeth! This is a pleasant surprise. Me and Sid were just having a bite to eat in the back room. Didn't hear the doorbell. Sorry about that."

"You didn't hear the bell," Elizabeth said with a hint of disapproval, "because it isn't working properly. It might be a good idea to put that right, George. This is supposed to be a well-ordered establishment, is it not?"

"Oh, quite right, your ladyship. Quite right." George turned his face and blasted over his shoulder, "Sid! Get your lazy arse out here and mend this doorbell."

Elizabeth winced. "Thank you, George."

"My pleasure, your ladyship. Now, what can I do for you today?"

Elizabeth took the seat in front of the desk. "You can tell me how the investigation into Basil Thorncroft's murder is going."

George's expression immediately became guarded.

Sid appeared in the doorway just then, brandishing a screwdriver. "Why is it always me what has to mend things around here," he began, then his frown turned to a smile as he caught sight of Elizabeth. "What a pleasure it is to see you, your ladyship!"

Elizabeth nodded at him. "Likewise, Sid, I'm sure."

"I suppose you've come about that nasty business in one of your cottages—"

George cut him off with a loud clearing of his throat. "Get over to that door, Sid, and stop your blathering. I'm sure her ladyship has better things to do than listen to your gossip."

Quite the contrary, Elizabeth thought. She often uncovered far more information from Sid's careless prattle than George's cautiously measured answers to her questions. "Actually," she said, "I did rather want to know what's happening in the cottage. I need to rent it again as soon as possible, and Sadie will have to get in there to clean it up before we can show it to anyone. Do you happen to know when she'll be able to do that?"

Wearing his officious expression, George shuffled a few papers on his desk. "Well, now, I think that can be arranged. I'm told the investigation should be finished by tonight. I'd say that you should be able to clean the cottage tomorrow."

Elizabeth looked at him in pleased surprise. "That soon? I'd expected to wait much longer. Have you solved the case, then? You know who murdered Mr. Thorncroft?"

George avoided her gaze. "Not exactly, your ladyship."

"Oh. Well, then, have you found anything at all that might tell you what happened?"

"Not precisely, no."

She let out her breath in an impatient huff. "Then what *do* you know?"

George shook his head. "I'm sorry, Lady Elizabeth, but you know very well I can't discuss a murder case."

"Well, I do know the poor man was stabbed. That much I could see for myself."

"Yes, you're quite right, m'm. He was stabbed all right."

"With a knife, I presume?"

George gave her a tight nod.

"Has the knife been found?"

She received a negative shake in answer.

"Tell you what," Sid said from the front door, where he was studying a tangle of bare wires that protruded from the silent bell. "Whoever did it knew what he was doing, all right. Weren't no amateur did this one. Stabbed the poor bugger right through the heart. Never had a chance, he didn't."

"Shut up, Sid," George growled.

Elizabeth digested this news, then asked, with little hope of an answer, "Does the inspector have any idea of a motive?"

"That's a laugh," Sid said. "We ain't seen hide nor hair of the inspector in months. I reckon he's given up police work and hasn't bothered to tell anyone, that's what I think."

George snorted. "Full of brilliant ideas, aren't you. Just shut your trap and get on with the job."

Elizabeth's brow wrinkled in a puzzled frown. "How can you be finished with a murder investigation without a police inspector?"

"The inspector's not handling this one," George said. He was beginning to look agitated, a sure sign that he was doing his best to keep something from her.

Elizabeth's interest sharpened. "He's not? Then who is handling it?"

George pinched his lips before answering her. "The case has been taken over higher up."

"Higher up? Whatever does that mean?"

"It's secret—" Sid began, but George cut him off.

"It's a big secret," he said, giving Sid a murderous look. "Can't tell you, I'm afraid, your ladyship."

Elizabeth sighed. "George, a tenant of mine has been brutally murdered. An innocent man struck down for no apparent reason. I —"

"That's what you think," Sid muttered.

Elizabeth twisted around in her chair to look at him. "I beg your pardon?"

"He said it's hard to think," George said, glowering at his partner. "Sid, get down to the ironmonger's and buy a new bell for that door. I'm sick of watching you fiddle with it."

"That's all the blinking gratitude I get," Sid mumbled. He reached for the constable's helmet hanging from a nail on the wall and crammed it on his head. "Get this, get that. Anyone would think I was your flipping slave instead of your partner."

George half rose from his chair with a threatening frown.

"All right, all right, I'm going." Sid saluted Elizabeth. "Ta ta, your ladyship. Nice to see you, I'm sure."

As the door closed behind him, Elizabeth rose, too. "Well, George, if that's all you can tell me, I suppose I'd better be off. You say it will be all right to clean the cottage tomorrow, then?"

George scrambled to his feet. "Yes, m'm. I was told the investigation would be completed as of today."

She smiled hopefully at him. "I suppose you can't tell me who told you that?"

George lifted his shoulders in a helpless shrug.

"I didn't think so." She crossed the room to the door. "Thank you, George." She turned to go, then turned back. "Can you at least tell me if the Americans have anything to do with it?"

George shook his head.

"No, they don't have anything to do with it? Or no, you can't tell me?"

George spread his fingers and wagged his hand from side to side.

Elizabeth sighed. "Good day, George." She closed the door carefully behind her, then crossed the pavement to her motorcycle. In the distance she saw Sid pedaling furiously up the street on his bicycle. If she was going to find out anything about this puzzle, her best bet was Sid's loose tongue.

With a hefty kick of the pedal, she fired the engine, and charged up the road after him.

CHAPTER

❀ 4 ❀

It took Elizabeth only a moment or two to catch up with Sid. Pulling up alongside of him, she turned off her engine.

Sid grinned at her. "Wouldn't mind having an engine like that on me bicycle, your ladyship. It would save a lot of wear and tear on me old legs, that's for sure."

"I'm sure it would. Though surely a motorcar would be even better?" Elizabeth pulled off her goggles, taking care not to dislodge her hat. The rain had eased somewhat since that morning, but the wind still chased heavy clouds across the sky, and it was only a matter of time before the next deluge.

Sid followed her glance at the clouds. "Might be a lot

38

drier, I reckon. This uniform gets heavy when it's wet. Which is most of the time lately."

Elizabeth tucked her scarf more securely into the neck of her coat. "We do seem to have had more than our share of storms in the past week or two."

"No sign of them letting up, neither."

Deciding that this was enough small talk, Elizabeth jumped right in. "Sid, what did you mean by that remark about Basil Thorncroft?"

Sid looked wary. "What remark was that, then, your ladyship?"

"When I mentioned that he was an innocent man, struck down for apparently no reason, I believe your words were, 'That's what you think,' or something like that."

"Oh." Sid appeared to be struggling with his conscience. After a moment or two, he blurted out, "I only meant he was a big drinker, that's all. He was always down the Tudor Arms, knocking them back. Drank like a fish, he did."

"I see." Elizabeth turned this over in her mind. "I was under the impression he didn't get out much. Did you see him drinking with anyone else?"

Sid shook his head. "No, never. These artist chaps can be a bit standoffish anyway, if you get my meaning."

"I suppose so." Elizabeth started her engine again, and shouted over the muffled roar. "Thank you, Sid. I enjoyed talking to you."

"You, too, your ladyship." Sid touched his helmet and pedaled off, leaving Elizabeth to gaze after him.

Usually Sid could be counted on to let slip what George tried so hard to keep from her. Either he was telling the truth, and his remark was nothing more than a simple observation, or whatever it was George didn't want her to know was far too important for even Sid to divulge.

In which case, Elizabeth vowed as she roared up the High Street, she would not rest until she knew what exactly it was that was such a big secret.

Polly stared at the sheaf of papers in front of her, the figures on them blurred by the tears she fought to hold back. She'd finally seen Sam in the great hall after days of hanging around the east wing, where the Americans were billeted.

It hadn't been easy finding excuses to be in that part of the mansion, and she'd had to offer her help to Sadie to make it seem like she belonged there.

She must love Sam a lot, she reflected, brushing her eyes with her sleeve. Cleaning the loos never had been her favorite job, and now that she was Lady Elizabeth's assistant, she'd thought she was finished with scrubbing toilet bowls. Still, it had been worth it to see Sam again.

At least it would have been, if he'd acted pleased to see her. It broke her heart to see the ugly scars on his face, but only because it reminded her of the dreadful pain he'd been in at the hospital. He still looked gorgeous to her, and he always would.

She'd tried to tell him that just now, but he'd cut her off without even so much as a smile. Ever since the accident he'd refused to look her in the eye. If he'd just look at her, maybe she could tell if he'd really broken up with her because she'd lied about her age and was too young for him, which was what he'd told her, or if it was his scars making him feel like a freak, like the doctor said. If only she could know for sure that Sam still loved her, she'd do anything in the world to make him believe he was still the gorgeous, exciting man she'd loved from the first moment she'd set eyes on him.

A tear splashed onto the page in front of her, smudging the neat figures. She reached for the blotter and dabbed at the spot, then dipped the pen into the inkwell before writing in the figures again. At that moment the door opened, and a cheerful, well-scrubbed face peered around it.

"You all right?" Sadie Buttons demanded. "You look as if you've lost a shilling and found a farthing."

Polly sniffed, and dabbed at her nose with her sleeve. "I'm all right. If you're looking for her ladyship, she's gone into town."

Sadie jerked her head in a nod and stepped into the room, closing the door behind her. "I was looking for you." She plonked herself down on a chair and stretched out her legs in front of her. The long pinafore she wore reached almost to her shoes, and she hooked it up over her knees. "Cor blimey, me feet hurt. There's a lot of stairs in this blooming house."

"I know." Polly pulled a face. "I've done enough of them in my time."

"Yeah, I know." Sadie looked around at the dark-paneled walls of the office. "You like working in here?"

"I love it," Polly said truthfully. "It's much better than being a housemaid." She saw Sadie's expression change and added hastily, "Not that there's anything wrong with being a housemaid. After all, I was one meself for a while. I just like doing all the book work and talking on the telephone, making appointments for her ladyship and answering people's questions for her. Makes me feel important."

Sadie looked unimpressed. "Yeah, well, I can't see me sitting on me bot all day. I need to be out 'n about." She peered at Polly across the antique oak desk. "So what's all that about with you and that GI then? You two having a fling or something?"

Polly stared hard at the rows of figures in front of her. "We was going out for a few months. Then we had a really bad accident in a Jeep and it messed up his face and now he won't have nothing to do with me."

"Ah." Sadie nodded wisely. "More 'n likely he's afraid you think he's ugly now. He probably thinks you wouldn't want to kiss him now he's all banged up."

Polly gazed hopefully at her. "That's what the doctor said. You really think that's it?"

Sadie nodded so hard the bunches of brown hair on either side of her face bounced up and down. " 'Course I do! Seen it a dozen times, I have. These air force blokes coming back from the Battle of Britain with their faces all burned up—'orrible, some of them look. They don't think a woman's ever going to look at them again, leave alone want to kiss them. Silly buggers. Don't they know that women don't care about looks if they love the bloke?" Sadie snorted in disgust. "Men! They're all blinking alike."

Polly felt a stirring of hope. "So what do I do about it, then? How can I make Sam believe I still love him even with his scars?"

"Give him time." Sadie pushed herself up from the chair. "He'll come around, you'll see. Just don't give up on him. In the meantime, you look like you could do with some cheering up. How about coming down the Tudor Arms with me tonight? Take your mind off things. What with that blinking murder in the lane and your Sam giving you the cold shoulder, no wonder you look so miserable."

Polly stacked the papers into a neat pile while she thought about it. "I don't know," she said at last. "I haven't been down the pub since the accident. It doesn't seem right somehow, going down there without Sam being there."

"There's no harm in going down there for a drink. You don't have to talk to no Yanks or nothing." Sadie leaned her palms on the desk and stared earnestly into Polly's face. "Come on, it will do you good. They've got a new barmaid down there. Her name's Bridget, and she's full of spit and vinegar. She makes Alfie the barman look like a blinking statue. You should hear the way she talks to the blokes down there. Won't take no funny stuff from 'em. You'll like her. She got them all going last night. The whole pub was singing. You know how dead it used to be in the Arms on a Sunday night? Well, it ain't no more. Sunday night is song night every week now." She flung out her arm as if she were announcing to a big audience. "With Prissy Priscilla at the piano!"

Polly's eyes widened. "Priscilla Pierce is playing the piano at the pub?"

Sadie burst out laughing. "You sound like a tongue twister. Yeah, Priscilla's playing for the song night. Bit of a ninny, she is, but can she whack them ivories! Got the whole place shaking, she has. You gotta go down there next Sunday."

Tempted in spite of herself, Polly murmured, "Sounds like this new barmaid is livening up the place a bit."

"You bet she is." Sadie crossed the room to the door. "You coming tonight or not? Probably won't be much singing, but we could play darts with the blokes. It's better than sitting around moping, ain't it?"

It certainly was. Maybe it wouldn't be the same without Sam, but Polly was getting awfully tired of sitting in front of the fireplace all evening listening to boring stuff on the wireless. "All right, I'll go. Mind if I bring my sister with me? She hasn't been out much lately, neither."

"Not at all! The more the merrier. See you tonight, then." With a wave of her hand, Sadie vanished.

Now that she'd made up her mind, Polly was actually looking forward to the evening. Beginning to feel better already, she picked up her pen again, dipped it into the inkwell, and began to write.

It had been a long day, and Elizabeth was only too thankful to settle onto her comfy wicker couch in the conservatory and enjoy a glass of her favorite sherry before dinner. She had invited the major to join her—a pleasure that was fast becoming a dangerous habit.

The more she saw of Earl Monroe, the more intensely aware she was of her growing affection for him. At first, she had alleviated her guilt by assuring herself it was simply a deep friendship she felt for the handsome major, but nowadays it had become difficult to contain her wild excitement every time she waited for his arrival.

Such as right now, with a glass of sherry trembling in her hand. It didn't seem to matter that Earl had a wife and children waiting for him in America. They didn't seem real to her. Or perhaps she didn't want to think of them as being flesh and blood people. Earl's family. Perhaps she should make them real in her mind. Maybe then she could get over this silly crush she had on him, before she made an unfortunate slip and he realized how she felt about him.

Once that happened, she was quite sure it would change things forever between them. He would feel obligated to keep some distance between them, and that would break her heart, even while she applauded his integrity. No, she could not let that happen. Right now she was content to enjoy whatever brief moments she had with him and put off the eventual heartbreak when this delightful relationship came to its inevitable end.

What she should do, she decided with some reluctance, was encourage Earl to talk about his family. That way they would become more established in her mind. While undoubtedly it would hurt to listen to him talk of his loved ones, it might help ease the burden of guilt that plagued her every time she imagined herself in his arms. Which was happening entirely too often these days.

He chose that moment to arrive, tapping on her door and waiting for her response before his ruggedly handsome face appeared in the doorway. "You started without me?" He advanced into the room, encouraging her heart to beat a rapid tattoo against her ribs. "I guess you need something to steady your nerves after the lousy shock you had this morning."

"It's a good excuse, anyway." She smiled at him, and gestured at the bottle of his favorite scotch. "Help yourself."

"Thanks, I could use a belt as well. I've been out on the abandoned runway at the base all afternoon. We're thinking of building a rec hall on it for the guys, since we're not using it for anything else. They need somewhere to let off steam, and a fast game of squash would go a long way."

"I'm sure it would. I've never played the game, but I understand it's quite energetic."

"Nothing you couldn't handle."

He grinned at her, and she gave a little gasp as he withdrew his hand from behind his back and held out a small package wrapped in colorful paper. "What's this?"

"Just wanted to thank you for your hospitality to a lonely soldier."

She took the package from him, terribly afraid she was going to cry. "How sweet! But entirely unnecessary. After all, you more than repay me with all that brandy from the base. I think Violet and Martin have you written into their wills."

He laughed, much to her intense pleasure. Sitting down opposite her, he said lightly, "I kinda figured Violet disapproved of me."

She began unwrapping the gift with nervous fingers. "She disapproves of me spending so much time with you. There's a difference."

"That bothers you?"

She paused to look at him. "Not at all. Does it you?"

He shrugged. "I wouldn't want to jeopardize your reputation."

"That wouldn't bother me, either." The words were out before she could stop them.

Flustered, she watched him raise his eyebrows. "Well, well, well! Don't tell me that stiff British control is beginning to crack a little?"

Thoroughly mortified, she hurried to rectify her mistake. "Not at all. I merely meant that if people choose to misconstrue our relationship, the problem is theirs, not mine."

His eyes crinkled at the edges, though she saw a certain regret in them that stopped her breath. "Always the lady. I might have known. Too bad."

Unable to answer him just then, she concentrated on her gift. She could barely get the package unwrapped, her fingers trembled so much. Finally she reached a small box and opened it. Inside lay a miniature oval frame, just the size of a small photograph. "Oh, how exquisite!" Elizabeth studied the tiny flowers etched into the silver. "Is it antique?"

"I guess so. I found it in a secondhand shop in North Horsham. How'd you know that?"

Elizabeth cradled the frame in her palm. "These miniatures were very popular in the Victorian era. My mother carried one with her all the time. It was lost when she was killed in the Blitz."

"I'm sorry—I didn't mean to—"

"Oh, no, it's all right!" She gazed at him, putting her heart in her eyes. "It's perfect. I adore it. Thank you so much."

He nodded, looking relieved. "I thought you might want to put a picture of Gracie and George in there."

She didn't say so, but she'd already made up her mind which picture she'd place in the precious gift. Something far more special than a picture of the dogs he'd given her. Much as she loved them.

No, the photograph that would be housed in this beautiful frame was one taken earlier that summer at a garden fete for the local newspaper. A photograph of her and Earl, standing together, smiling in the warm sunlight of the vicarage gardens. The only picture she would ever have of the two of them together. It was all she would have left after he'd gone back to his family.

Carefully she placed the frame on the small table at her side, then took a long sip of sherry. She waited until he'd poured himself a glass and had settled back in his chair, before saying deliberately, "I was wondering if you've heard from your family lately?"

His start of surprise unnerved her. "Not for a while. Beverly isn't much of a letter writer, and I reckon the kids are pretty busy with their lives right now."

She really didn't want to do this, but she made herself go on. "What are your children doing these days? You don't talk about them very much. Are they still in school?"

He gave her an odd look. "Well, Marcia's graduated. She's working for a small theater company. Brad's in his senior year at high school."

"Your daughter is interested in acting? What fun!"

"Actually she's more interested in set design. Not too many women are in that field. It'll be a challenge for her."

"I can well imagine. What about your son? Does he have any plans after he leaves school?"

"College, I guess. I haven't had much chance to discuss his future with him."

Elizabeth took another careful sip of her sherry. "It must be awfully hard on your wife, trying to manage their lives without you."

Earl shrugged. "Beverly's a capable woman. She's always had a good handle on the kids. Far more than I have."

Hearing his note of regret, Elizabeth hurried to reassure him. "I'm sure that's not true. Mothers have more time to spend with their children, but it's the father to whom they look up and respect."

Earl uttered a somewhat bitter laugh. "Not my kids. I sometimes wonder if they know I even exist."

Uncomfortable at opening this can of worms, Elizabeth sought to change the subject. "I was at the police station today. I wanted to know when we could go in and clean the cottage. George was acting very strangely. I think there's something more to this murder business than he wants to tell me."

If Earl was taken aback by her abrupt switch in the conversation, he kept it to himself. "I thought he was always closed-mouthed about an investigation."

"Well, that, yes. But there's something else he said—

about it all being a very big secret. Even Sid was reluctant to tell me anything, and usually I can get almost anything out of him." She stood her glass on the table. "You don't suppose an American is involved in some way, do you?"

Earl frowned. "Did George say that?"

"That's just it. George wouldn't tell me anything. He didn't deny or confirm it."

"Could be he doesn't know."

"Well, yes, that could be it, I suppose. He did say the case had been taken over by someone higher up."

"Scotland Yard?"

She sighed. "I'm not sure what he meant. He said the inspector wouldn't be handling it. I don't know if he meant that someone with more authority in Scotland Yard would be handling it, or if someone else entirely was taking over the case. It's all very puzzling."

"I hope you're not thinking of doing some investigating on your own? You've had some pretty close calls in the past. I was hoping you'd given up playing detective."

She smiled at him. "I don't plan on getting involved with this one. I just hope that all this talk of handing over the case doesn't mean the murderer will slip through their fingers. One can't let people run around stabbing whomever they please. Someone has to pay for the death of poor Mr. Thorncroft. But usually George and Sid manage to bumble their way through an investigation without too much assistance from the inspector."

"Thanks largely to your efforts," Earl said dryly.

"And yours," she reminded him.

He grinned. "We do make a real good team, don't we?"

She smiled back. "We certainly do."

His grin faded, and an expression she couldn't quite interpret crept into his eyes. "Elizabeth, what were all those questions about before?"

She pretended not to understand him. "Questions?"

"About my family. Is something bothering you? Something you want to know?"

She managed a light laugh. "Not at all. I was just being polite, that's all. It's good manners to inquire after someone's loved ones."

He continued to gaze at her with that odd expression. She wondered if the room had suddenly grown warm, or if it was her discomfort making her feel so breathless.

When at last he spoke, she was unprepared for his unsettling words. "Elizabeth, my wife and I have not been on very good terms for a good many years. I'd rather not go into the sordid details right now, and I'm not real sure this is what you wanted to know, but I'm telling you anyway. Just in case it was."

Try as she might, she could not think of a single word in reply.

CHAPTER
❀ 5 ❀

There were a million things Elizabeth wanted to say in that moment, yet she could say none of them. She sensed that this was some kind of turning point in her relationship with Earl, and she was terrified of destroying the wonderful, tantalizing, and so very fragile thread that had bonded them up until now.

She didn't want anything to change, and yet she did. She wanted what she couldn't have, and she didn't want to lose what they already had. Right at that moment she wished like hell that he had never walked into her life and disrupted it so. Just when she thought she'd settled her mind and her future.

"Thank you for telling me," she said at last. "I'm so very sorry your marriage isn't going well. Perhaps, when this war is over . . ." She'd been going to say that she hoped he and his wife would be able to sort things out, but as she reached for her glass, her shaky hand misjudged the distance. The glass tipped, spilling sherry onto the carpet as it fell. With a little cry, she made a grab for it. At the same time Earl reached for it, too. Instead of grasping the glass, his hand closed over hers instead.

She refused to look at him, afraid of what she might see in his eyes. It wouldn't take very much encouragement right then to ignore all the proprieties and grasp the opportunity that presented itself with such exquisite promise.

Somehow she found the strength to regain her composure. With a little laugh, she pulled her hand free and picked up the empty glass. "How terribly clumsy of me. Violet will be most upset with me. I'd better get something to mop this up before it stains the carpet."

She rose, and he stood up with her. "Don't be afraid of me, Elizabeth," he said softly.

She made herself look at him, and her heart turned over at his expression. "Never. I trust you more than any man I've ever known."

He winced. "That could backfire on me. Maybe I'd better leave while I'm ahead." He reached for her hand and brought it to his mouth. "Good night, sweet lady."

Her lips trembled on the words. "Good night, Earl." She watched him leave, her heart aching for what might have been. For a heady moment or two she'd actually allowed herself to believe that her fantasies could come true. But the truth, painful as it was, stared her in the face. No matter how unsatisfactory Earl's relationship was with his wife, the fact remained that he was married. And no self-respecting lady of the manor dare tamper with that.

As she crossed the room to the door, she felt the weight of her frustration heavy on her heart. There were times, indeed, when she cursed her birthright, and the burdens it brought with it.

"Aw, come on, Marlene, don't be a bad sport." Polly sat on the edge of the bed while her sister pulled on a pair of filmy nylon stockings. "We haven't been down the Arms in ages. Whatcha want to go out with this bloke tonight for, anyway? You don't even know him."

"I know him well enough to know he's got good breeding and money," Marlene muttered. "That's a lot better than the slobs you meet down the pub. He's even got a car. I've never been with a bloke with a car before." She twisted her head around as far as it would go. "Are me seams straight? I can't tell from here."

"Yeah, they're all right." Polly wriggled impatiently on the bed. "He can't be that rich. Where's he come from, anyway?"

"He said he lives in Surrey, right near London."

"What's he do? Why isn't he in the army? What's he doing in Sitting Marsh if he's got all this money?"

"I don't know and I don't care."

"You don't know nothing about him, do you."

"He doesn't like talking about himself. He just wants to talk about me, and that suits me just fine as long as he gives me a good time." Marlene picked up a lipstick and peered at her face in the mirror. "Wonder if I should put Vaseline on me eyebrows?"

"Nah, makes you look like you forgot to wash properly." Polly started pulling the pins out of her hair. "I just don't see how any English bloke could be better than the Yanks. I thought you liked the Yanks."

"I do." Marlene finished smoothing the bright red lipstick on her lips. "But there's no future in it, is there?"

Polly paused, her hand full of pins. "Whatcha mean, there's no future in it?"

"What I say." Marlene sat down next to her and slid her foot into a black platform shoe. "They're all going back to the States one day, aren't they. They're just playing with us over here. They know they can't get serious with us."

Polly did her best to ignore her pang of fear. "Some of them do. There's a lot of English girls what marry Yanks and go to America to live."

"Yeah, well, I don't know as if I'd want to go to America to live, anyway. All them big buildings and motorcars rushing about all over the place."

"It's not like that everywhere. They've got palm trees and beaches in Hollywood."

"That's what they show you in the films. Bet it's not really like that." Marlene pushed her toes into the other shoe. "Anyway, I've had it with the Yanks and their wandering hands. I'm going to find myself a nice British bloke, and if he's got money, so much the better." She nudged Polly in the arm. "You should see his car. All black shiny leather inside. Real posh it is. Can't hardly hear the engine when you're sitting in it. It's like riding on a cloud it is."

"I'd rather ride in a Jeep," Polly said stiffly.

"No you wouldn't. Look at how your makeup and hair gets all messed up in the wind and the rain. I can step into Pete's car and get out of it looking just as perfect as when I got in."

Polly snorted. "Got a blinking big opinion of yourself, haven't you? Anyway, there's a lot more important things to know about a bloke than his bloomin' car."

"Like what?"

"Like how he treats you, and how good he kisses."

"Well, I don't know how good he kisses"—Marlene got up from the bed—"but you can bet I'm going to find out. In the comfy back seat of a posh car." She smoothed her hands down her tight black skirt. "How do I look?"

"You look all right. I just wish you was coming down the pub with me instead of riding around in some toff's car. Sadie says that the Arms is really lively now that the new barmaid is working there. You'd have a lot more fun."

"You're just jealous you don't have a bloke with a car." Marlene peered in the mirror again and fluffed her hair. "Though mind you, I almost got done in this morning."

Polly stared at her. "Go on! What happened?"

"Well, Pete was driving awfully fast up the road, and when he saw me sitting there, he had to swerve and he ended up in the ditch. He made me sit at the wheel while he pushed the car out. He showed me how to steer it and everything, but he forgot to tell me not to step too hard on the pedal. I shot out backward and almost went over the cliff. Thought I was a goner I did."

"Oh, gawd. What did he say, then?"

"Not much. It shook him up a bit and he said he was really sorry."

"I should blinking think he would be sorry. He could have killed you. If you'd gone over that cliff, you'd be bloody dead by now."

Marlene smiled at herself in the mirror. "Well, I'm not, am I. And I'm going to make sure he makes up for it tonight."

Polly pulled the last of the pins from her hair, then slid off the bed. "Well, I still think you'd have more fun down the pub. I'd better get ready if I'm going to meet Sadie. I hate walking down the coast road in the rain. I look such a mess by the time I get there."

Marlene peered at her alarm clock on the bedside table. "If you can be ready in ten minutes, I'll ask Pete to drop you off there. Save you getting wet."

"I'll be ready." Polly flew across the room, stopping only long enough to give her sister a quick hug. "Thanks ever so much, Marl."

"Well, it will give you a chance to meet Pete. You can tell me what you think of him."

"I will," Polly promised, then dashed off to get ready before Marlene could change her mind.

She was anxious to meet her sister's new boyfriend. She wasn't at all sure she liked the idea of Marlene tearing around in a car with a bloke what drove too fast, and almost got her killed. Ma would have a fit if she knew. Which was why she wasn't going to tell her. But she was going to tell Pete whatever-his-name to be more careful while he was with her sister. 'Cos if anything happened to Marlene, neither she nor Ma would ever get over it.

Sobered by the thought, she dabbed makeup on her face with far less care than if she'd been getting ready to go out with Sam. The evening was turning out worse than she thought. No Sam and no Marlene. Life just wasn't as much fun anymore.

The sound of raised voices above the blaring music in the saloon bar of the Tudor Arms just about blew Polly's eardrums when she walked in there half an hour later. Sadie was already seated at the bar, and she waved a frantic arm the moment she saw Polly walk through the door.

Polly had to fight her way through a group of soldiers, all of whom greeted her with whistles and cheeky remarks as she pushed past them to get to the bar.

Sadie grinned at her as she emerged, red-faced, from the rowdy group. "Thought you'd got lost."

She lifted her handbag from the barstool next to her and Polly climbed onto it. "I had to wait for my sister's new boyfriend to give me a lift, didn't I. I didn't want to get soaked on me way down."

"I know." Sadie shook her head and sprayed drops of water over the counter. "My hair still hasn't dried."

Polly stared around at people jostling for space around the tables. "What's going on? Is it someone's birthday? I've never seen it this crowded down here on a Monday night."

"You can thank Bridget for that. Here she is now." Sadie waved her arm at the woman approaching them behind the bar. "Bridget! Come and meet me mate, Polly."

Polly stared at the new barmaid. She was about Ma's age, and her flaming red hair was a frizzy mess. How Marlene would love to get her hands on that lot! Bridget's bosoms were so big they rested on the counter like two footballs stuffed in a shirt, and her arms were as thick as pillar-boxes. Sadie was a bit on the hefty side, but she looked skinny next to Bridget. No wonder this new barmaid didn't take no nonsense off the blokes. She looked a lot tougher than some of them.

"Pleased to meet you, Polly." Bridget flicked a mock salute at her. "What's your pleasure?"

"I'll have a gin and orange." Polly watched her half-a-crown disappear into Bridget's massive hand. "Blimey," she whispered to Sadie as the burly barmaid moved off to serve someone else, "She's a right bruiser. I wouldn't want to get on the wrong side of her."

Sadie laughed. "Bridget's all right. She's a good giggle, she is. The blokes all like her. You should hear some of the jokes she tells. Make your ears curl up. Got a terrific voice, too. You should hear her on song night. Get's the whole place jumping up and down, she does. Just like a good old London pub."

Polly sipped her gin. "Is that where she comes from? London?"

Sadie shrugged. "Don't know. She never said. So, what's your sister's boyfriend like?"

"Not bad." Polly took another sip of her drink. "Good-looking bloke and he drives a really posh car. Marlene always wanted a rich bloke. Looks like she's got one this time. Although . . ." She let her voice trail off, not sure what she wanted to say next.

"Although what?"

Polly hesitated, then said carefully, "I don't know what it was, but there's something . . . weird about him. He kept asking me all these questions about Sam, and the Americans staying at the manor, and what the local girls said about the Yanks. He even asked me what Sam and I talked about when we were alone. I wanted to tell him to mind his own business. Made me feel creepy, he did."

"What does Marlene say about him?"

Polly hunched her shoulders. "All she sees is his nice clothes and fancy car. She almost got killed in that car this morning." Briefly she described Marlene's narrow escape. "I just don't have a very good feeling about him, that's all," she finished.

"Sure you're not jealous?" Sadie asked with a laugh.

"About him? Not on your life. He's nothing next to my Sam." Polly twisted her glass around in her fingers. "I just wish Sam was here now. I miss him so much."

Sadie patted her arm. "He'll come around, you'll see. Like I said, he just needs some time. Come on, drink up, and we'll go show those boys over there how a Londoner plays darts."

Polly finished her drink, though for once it failed to warm her inside. She wasn't sure if it was missing Sam that gave her that cold feeling, or Marlene's new boyfriend. Whatever it was, she just wished this evening was over and she could go home. She should have known she wouldn't have a good time without Sam. She should never have come, that was for sure. It was going to be a very long night.

The old iron bell at the front door clanged several times the next morning before Violet finally gave up hope of Martin answering it. Grumbling to herself, she dusted the flour from her hands onto her flowing white apron, then trudged up the stairs to answer the door herself.

Martin was probably upstairs, talking to an imaginary Lord Wellsborough. Ever since the butler had insisted that he'd seen the ghost of the dead earl walking through the great hall, he'd spent the major portion of his day up there.

Violet could never understand why he would prefer the damp, drafty halls to the cozy warmth of the kitchen, but she was thankful his fanciful notions kept him from being underfoot. Except at times like this when she had to leave pastry getting warm on the table to do his job for him.

She'd promised Lizzie that she'd help out when she could. They both knew that Martin couldn't handle the job anymore, but as long as he was alive, he'd have a home in the manor, and Lizzie was determined he'd never know they were managing his duties behind his back. Though there were times when Violet could swear he knew what they were up to, and just didn't want to admit he was getting senile.

Breathing a little heavier with the exertion, she reached the top of the stairs and hurried to the front door just as the bell clanged one more time. The ringing in her ears rattled her, and she glared at the woman who hovered on the front step. "Yes? What can I do for you?"

The woman backed away a step or two. She wore a scarf wrapped around her flushed face, from which thin strands of wet gray hair hung dismally over her eyes. "Oh, I'm sorry, I was expecting the gentleman to answer the door."

Violet raised her sparse eyebrows. "Gentleman? There's no gentleman living here. Unless you mean one of the Americans."

The woman looked confused. She clutched the lapels of her shapeless tweed coat closer to her throat. "American? Oh, no, this gentleman was definitely English. Rather elderly, with glasses?"

"Oh, you mean Martin?"

"Yes!" The woman looked relieved. "He usually opens the door."

Violet narrowed her eyes. "Usually? You've been here before?"

The woman nodded. "Yes, a few times. The gentleman . . . Mr.—?"

"Martin," Violet said bluntly. "He's the butler."

"Oh!" Now the woman seemed confused. "I didn't know. I'm not from these parts."

"I guessed that much." Violet eyed the bulging shopping bag the woman carried. Her curiosity was killing her. Martin never had visitors. At least as far as she knew. "He's somewhere in the house. I'll see if I can find him. It might take a while, if you want to wait?" She nodded at the bag. "Or I can take that, if you've got something for him?"

The woman clutched the bag to her chest as if afraid Violet would snatch it from her grasp. "Oh, no, it's just that Mr., er, Martin buys his raffle tickets from me. My name is Beatrice Carr and I come in from North Horsham on the bus now and again. I like the ride and I sell lots of raffle tickets here in the village."

"Raffle tickets?" Violet stared at the woman. She'd heard it all now. "Martin was buying *raffle tickets*? What for?"

Obviously uncomfortable now, Beatrice backed up another step. "Oh, various things. It's all for the war effort, you see. Perhaps I should come back another time."

"Perhaps you should." Violet folded her arms. "I'll tell Martin you were here."

Beatrice nodded, backed away, nodded again, then turned and fled down the steps. Violet waited until she'd reached the bottom one then called out, "Just a minute!"

The woman turned, her face alight with hope. "Yes?"

"Did he ever win anything?"

Hope died on the creased face. "No, not yet. But I'm sure he will."

Violet thinned her lips. "That's what I thought." She slammed the door and dropped the heavy latch in place. Raffle tickets, indeed. Whatever next. Her forehead creased in a frown. Martin never spent money on anything that wasn't an absolute necessity. Not that he got paid much anyway, since Lizzie had lost all her money to that useless sod of a husband, but what little he had was carefully hoarded away. He was always going on about saving for his old age, as if he couldn't tell he was blinking ancient already.

Violet paused on the stairs as a thought hit her. On the other hand, Martin could have realized his time was running out and decided to fritter away his life savings. If so, she needed to have a stern word with him. The sooner the better, too, before some money-grubbing old woman like Beatrice Carr got her hands on it.

Arriving back in the kitchen, Violet was surprised to see Sadie huddled in front of the glowing coals in the stove. The huge furnace heated the water for the kitchen and bathrooms, and had to be kept alight, no matter how warm the kitchen became. Right now, what with all the recent storms coming in off the ocean, the winds were cool enough to keep the room at a reasonable temperature without opening the windows. Even so, it wasn't cold enough to seek warmth from the stove.

Violet felt a touch of apprehension as she studied Sadie's bowed back. "So what's wrong with you, then? Not ill, are you?"

Sadie jumped as if she'd been prodded with a rake. "No, I'm not ill." She twisted around, and her brown eyes looked huge in her white face. "Her ladyship wants me to go down and clean the cottage."

Violet glanced at the clock on the wide mantelpiece. "Well, you'd better get a move on, then. It's almost time to start on the lavatories."

Sadie looked as if she was about to burst into tears, which was very strange. The housemaid was usually full of spunk. Sometimes too much, in Violet's opinion. Poor Martin did his best to stay out of her way, seeing as how she was always trying to jolly him up, as she called it. Which could explain why he was lurking about upstairs instead of answering the door. Right now, though, Sadie looked as if she could do with some jollying up herself.

"What's the matter with you?" Violet demanded, beginning to feel irritated. Her pastry was still lying like wet rubber on the table, and if it got any warmer, she'd have to chuck it and start again. Which would mean they'd be short on the lard ration that week.

"I can't do it," Sadie said, in a voice that sounded quite different from her usual bombastic tone.

Violet folded her arms. "You can't do what?"

"I can't clean that cottage."

"Why the bloody blazes can't you?"

"Because it's evil, that's what." Sadie lifted her chin as her tone became more belligerent. "Everyone what stays in there gets bleeding murdered and I'm not going to be the next one. The devil's got a hand in this, you mark my words."

Violet sighed. "Only one person's ever been murdered there, and they'll find the culprit before he does it again. What makes you think he'd be after you, anyway?"

"Her ladyship almost died down there, too. Why would anyone kill that artist bloke, anyway? He never did nothing to hurt no one."

"You don't know that." Violet stomped over to the table and glared at her gray-looking pastry. "No one knows what he got up to before he came down here to paint."

"Well, whatever the reason, I ain't going into that cottage again until they know why he died and who did it. Even if I lose me job. So there."

Violet floured her hands, then picked up the pastry and balled it. She was tempted to tell Sadie to pack her things. She had no time to listen to hysterics about the devil, or anything else. On the other hand, it had taken Lizzie six months to find a suitable housemaid. Right now they couldn't afford to start looking all over again.

The problem was, the cottage had to be cleaned as soon as possible, because they couldn't afford to leave it empty, either. With a groan of disgust, she threw down the pastry and attacked it fiercely with her rolling pin. "All right," she muttered. "As soon as I get this pie in the oven, I'll come down with you and help you clean it. The devil knows better than to tangle with me."

She waited in a tense silence for Sadie to give her an argument, then let out a sigh of relief when the girl said reluctantly, "All right. I'll get the buckets ready."

Violet straightened her back as the door closed behind Sadie. Devil, indeed. What nonsense these young people talked. She absolutely refused to acknowledge the tiny prick of fear she'd felt at Sadie's words. Load of nonsense. No such thing as the devil. Was there?

CHAPTER

❧ 6 ❧

"You're looking tired, Polly," Elizabeth observed as she watched the girl sort through a pile of papers to file. "Are you feeling all right?"

Polly seemed startled, but she smiled when she answered, "Oh, yes, m'm, I'm all right, really. I just didn't sleep well last night, that's all."

"Is something wrong?"

Polly looked as if she wasn't sure she wanted to answer, but then she laid the papers down on top of the file and came back to sit in front of Elizabeth's desk. "I got a lot on me mind, m'm. What with Sam ignoring me all the time, and now Marlene's new boyfriend."

Elizabeth put down the letter she'd been reading. Right now her assistant's problems were more important than a villager's concern about vague rumors of a factory being built in the area. "Marlene has a new boyfriend?"

"Yes, m'm. Pete Weston. I met him last night. He gave me a lift down to the Arms. Got a real posh car, he has. Marlene says he's rich."

"How nice." Aware that something was seriously bothering her young assistant, Elizabeth added gently, "Is that a bad thing?"

Polly gave her a troubled look. "Well, no, I s'pose not. It's just that he seems a bit weird, that's all. He kept asking me lots of questions about the Yanks and all that, and he drives too fast. He almost killed Marlene on the coast road."

"What?" Elizabeth stared at her in horror. "How on earth did that happen?"

"First of all he nearly run into her then he almost sent her over the cliff. See, m'm, Marlene ran into this broken beer barrel and . . ."

Elizabeth listened with some concern as Polly related the story of Marlene's near-disastrous attempt to drive the car. "Well, it does seem as if it was simply an accident," she said when Polly had finished. "When did all this happen?"

"Early yesterday morning. When Marlene was on her way to work. He gave her a lift to work then asked her out last night. She didn't get back until really late. Good job Ma was asleep, she'd have boxed her ears for coming in that late."

"Well, I'm sure you're worrying about nothing. Marlene strikes me as being a sensible young woman. I don't think she'd allow herself to be led astray by anyone, do you?"

Polly shrugged. "No telling what our Marlene will do if she thinks there's money in it. She's always liked nice

things and wishing she had pots of money. I wouldn't
worry about her so much if she knew more about this
bloke. The funny thing is, he wants to know everything
about her, and about me as well, but he hasn't told her
one thing about himself, except that he comes from Surrey
and he's staying at the pub. She doesn't even know what
he's doing in Sitting Marsh. Now I ask you, m'm, what
would someone like him want in a village like this? And
why isn't he in the army?"

"There could be lots of reasons. Something wrong with
his health, perhaps his job is more important, he may have
too many family members fighting overseas . . ."

"I bet having money had something to do with it," Polly
said, a trifle bitterly.

Elizabeth had to admit, there did seem to be an element
of mystery about the young man Polly described. Nevertheless, it was her sister's business with whom she kept
company, and the best thing she could do, Elizabeth decided, was try her best to alleviate Polly's concerns.

"Well, no doubt Marlene will find out what she needs
to know soon enough. After all, she came home safely
last night, didn't she? We can't always judge people by
appearances, and her boyfriend is probably quite respectable and trustworthy. It's up to Marlene to set the stan-
dards she wants. I'm sure she's quite capable of doing
that."

Looking less than reassured, Polly rose from her chair.
"I hope so. Anyway, I'd better get on with this filing. It
seems to grow faster than I can put it away. Thank you,
m'm. I do feel better now I've talked about it. I tell you,
though, Marlene missed a good time down at the pub last
night. That new barmaid they've got down there is a right
scream, she is."

Relieved that Polly appeared more cheerful, Elizabeth

folded the letter in half and slipped it back in its envelope while she listened to her assistant prattle on about her night in the Tudor Arms. "I shall have to go down there and meet the new barmaid," she said when Polly paused for breath. "In the meantime, I'm going into the village. I trust you can take care of things here until I get back?"

" 'Course I can, m'm." Polly gave one of her usual expansive grins. "I can manage very well, thank you. All this will be done before you get back."

"Thank you, Polly." Elizabeth crossed the room to the door, her thoughts echoing Polly's comments. Something kept repeating itself over and over, and as she hurried down the stairs to the main hallway, she kept worrying about it. In her mind's eye she saw a car early yesterday morning racing along the coast road in a great hurry.

Instead of heading for the front door, she crossed the wide entrance hall and ran lightly down the stairs to the kitchen. Violet was nowhere to be seen, much to her relief. She lifted the telephone, hoping that Polly wasn't talking on the extension. Quickly she dialed Dr. Sheridan's number.

The grating voice answered her on the first ring. After a brief greeting, Elizabeth wasted no time in coming to the point. "I was wondering, Doctor, as the medical examiner on the murder case yesterday—"

"I'm not the M.E. on the case," Dr. Sheridan said bluntly. "Even if I were, Lady Elizabeth, you know very well I couldn't tell you anything."

Elizabeth ignored that. She was much too interested in his first statement. "If you're not the medical examiner, then who is? I wasn't aware the police had another examiner."

"Nor was I." Dr. Sheridan paused, obviously put out by being usurped by an outsider. "I was told the case was out of my hands. Didn't even have the decency to tell me why."

"Who told you that?"

"Some chaps who arrived right in the middle of my preliminary. I was hustled out of there as if they were trying to keep it all a big secret. Bloody frustrating, if I may say so, your ladyship."

"You certainly may," Elizabeth murmured. *Secret.* There was that word again. It would seem that the constables were not the only ones to be kept in the dark. All very puzzling. Without much hope, she added, "I don't suppose you had time to determine the time of death?"

"All I can tell you is that it had to be somewhere between two and four hours before you discovered the body. I didn't get much chance to work on it. As I said, those London chappies didn't waste any time getting rid of me."

"London?"

Dr. Sheridan cleared his throat. "Well, they sounded as if they came from London. Beg your pardon, Lady Elizabeth, but I probably shouldn't be talking about it. I was told to keep my mouth shut. Rather forcefully, I might add."

"I understand, Doctor. Thank you for your help." She exchanged a pleasantry or two, then hung up. Something was definitely going on in Sitting Marsh. Something odd and more than a little disturbing. As lady of the manor, she had an obligation to see that the mysterious factor that had taken control of the investigation did not interfere with the lives and well-being of her tenants.

Somehow she would have to ferret out the big secret and find out why this was apparently no ordinary murder case, and just why a reclusive artist merited the attention of such illustrious investigators from London.

• • •

"Well, will you look at this!" Violet stood inside the tiny front room of the cottage and stared around in amazement. "Looks like someone's already cleaned it out." She turned to Sadie, who was hovering behind her with a look of sheer terror on her face. "I hope you're not playing some kind of joke on me, young lady. I won't stand for that."

"I didn't have nothing to do with it, honest. It's the devil what did it. I told you this place was evil."

"Stuff and nonsense." Violet headed determinedly toward the kitchen. "Just because this room is tidy doesn't mean the rest of the place . . ." Her voice trailed off as she surveyed the spotless counters and scrubbed floor. "Well, I'll be blowed." The front door key sat in the middle of the table, and she picked it up to slip it in her pocket.

"See?" Sadie's voice was a mere squeak. "I told you. I'm getting out of here." The buckets she held in each hand rattled as she stumbled over to the front door.

"Sadie Buttons! You stop right there!" Violet dug both hands in her hips. "You're not leaving until we've inspected every inch of this place."

The buckets crashed to the floor as Sadie spun around. "I'm not going one flipping step further, so there."

Violet huffed her displeasure. "I'm going upstairs to look at the bedrooms. You stay here until I get back." She left the girl shivering in the middle of the front room and hurried up the stairs. Not a speck of dust could be seen anywhere on the bedroom furniture, and every personal belonging had disappeared. Even the dresser drawers had been emptied and neatly lined with clean paper.

Shaking her head, Violet descended the stairs and went through the kitchen door into the small back garden. The only sign that the artist had ever lived at Number One,

Sandhill Lane, was a half-dozen paintings sticking out of the dustbin.

Shocked at such a dreadful waste of someone's talent, Violet approached the dustbin to investigate. Only one painting looked clean enough to be worth saving. It had been protected from the rest of the rubbish by the other paintings, all of which had been soiled.

Violet pulled it out and examined it. Not a mark on it anywhere. Nice painting, too. Must have been done from the cliffs. There was a small building that looked a lot like the Tudor Arms, and a red sun was setting down in the sea, with all the colors reflected on the waves. Too good a painting to be chucked away in the dustbin.

Violet tucked the canvas under her arm and went back inside. Sadie stood where she'd left her in the middle of the front room, looking for all the world as if she'd just wet her drawers. For someone who'd been bombed out of her house in the Blitz, Violet thought wryly, the girl was surprisingly skittish. Then again, some people would rather face a dozen of Hitler's bombs than one measly hint of ghosts and goblins. Not that she believed in such things, of course.

"Well," she said briskly, "whoever cleaned this place up did a good job. Almost as good as I would have done. Saved us a bit of work, anyway."

"The devil's work, if you ask me," Sadie muttered. "You mark my words."

"I'll mark something else if you don't stop whining about the devil." Violet marched briskly to the front door. "If it *was* the devil, you should be thanking him for doing your job for you."

The rattle of buckets told her Sadie had picked them up. She waited for the housemaid to scramble outside, then locked the cottage door again.

"What you got there?" Sadie demanded as Violet tucked the canvas under her arm.

"One of Mr. Thorncroft's paintings. I found it in the dustbin on the back porch."

"You're not taking it home with you!"

Sadie's face was white as a sheet. Violet almost felt sorry for the girl. " 'Course I am. It will look really nice in Lady Elizabeth's study." She held the painting up and studied it. "Come to think of it, I think this is the one her ladyship was talking about. Said she saw it on the easel when she found that poor man on the floor."

Sadie moaned. "You take that back to the manor and you'll bring us all bad luck. You see if you don't."

Violet decided that the cold shiver down her back was nothing more than the bite from the brisk sea wind. "Just stop your nonsense, Sadie. You're beginning to get on my nerves. Come on, let's get a move on. I want to get this painting home before it starts raining again."

Sadie glanced up at the threatening clouds. "It looks like it's going to pour any minute."

"Well, we'll take the shortcut, through the fields." Violet shoved the painting under her coat and marched off, determined not to let Sadie's silly superstitions bother her. Bad luck, indeed. As if they didn't have enough of it already, what with the money running out, and a murder in Sandhill Lane, just when they needed the rent the most.

Though she had to admit, she was glad they hadn't had to clean the cottage. Although she'd be the last to admit it, there was something really strange about that place. She only hoped that whoever rented it next didn't feel it, too.

Two to four hours, Elizabeth mused as she roared noisily down the hill toward the little town of Sitting Marsh. That would put the murder somewhere between four and eight o'clock that morning. More likely closer to eight o'clock, since Basil Thorncroft was fully dressed. Unless, of course, he was a very early riser.

Marlene opened the hairdressers' shop at eight o'clock every morning. Elizabeth knew that because her regular appointment at the Manor House with Marlene was at ten past seven, allowing the hairdresser to get back to the shop in time to open it for her first customer.

So that meant Marlene's new boyfriend, Pete Weston, would have been driving very fast along the coast road about the time the murder could have taken place. Most likely a simple coincidence, but nevertheless, a place to start.

Acting on an impulse, Elizabeth turned into Sandhill Lane. Judging from what she'd heard, the cottage had been thoroughly investigated by the "chappies" from London. Still, it wouldn't hurt to look in on Sadie. It would give her a good excuse to take a good long look around while she was there. There was always a chance that the hurried investigation might have resulted in something being missed.

She cut off the engine, leaving a deathly silence in the wake of the shattering roar. For a moment it seemed that nothing stirred in the calm solitude of the countryside. As she walked up the garden path to the tune of her scrunching footsteps, however, she could hear the faint chattering of birds in the sweeping branches of a willow, and the distant swish of ocean waves breaking on the sands beyond the cliffs.

This late in the year the roses had lost their power, but a faint remnant of their fragrance still lingered in the air. Such a charming cottage, she thought as she rattled the door handle. It was really too bad that it seemed destined

to have such a macabre history. Frowning, she realized
that the door was locked. She pulled off her leather glove
and raised her hand to rap the brass knocker.

Nothing but an eerie silence greeted her hollow sum-
mons. Concerned now, she peered into the side window.
Surely Sadie couldn't be finished cleaning yet? Squinting
to see inside the shadowed room, she stared at the
plumped-up cushions sitting neatly on the tweed sofa. She
could see quite clearly the reflection of a vase in the sur-
face of a highly polished table. Certainly everything appeared to be clean and tidy.

Impressed by the speedy work of her new housemaid,
Elizabeth straightened her back. It would seem that her
investigation of the cottage would have to wait until she
retrieved the key from Sadie. Not that she really expected
to find anything, anyway.

Intent on her thoughts, she failed to see the man waiting
at the gate for her until the very last minute. She started
quite violently before exclaiming, "Captain Carbunkle! I
didn't see you there."

The bewhiskered gentleman had the grace to look re-
morseful as he swung open the gate for her to pass
through. "So sorry, your ladyship. Didn't mean to startle
you. Heard the old motorcycle engine and guessed it was
you. Thought I'd toddle over to see if there's anything I
can do."

"That's awfully decent of you, Captain." It was Elizabeth's considered opinion that it was more curiosity than
chivalry that had enticed the retired sea captain to hover
around in wait of her, but her upbringing demanded that
she perish the uncharitable thought. "As a matter of fact,
I'd intended to look in on my housemaid. She was sent
down here to clean the cottage this morning. Apparently

she must have completed her task sooner than I'd anticipated."

The captain nodded his head long before she'd finished the sentence. "They left some time ago. Saw them toddle off across the fields." He waved a chubby arm in the direction of the manor.

"Them?" Elizabeth stared at him. "Are you saying someone was with Sadie?"

"Yes, m'm. Violet was with her. Had something tucked under her arm. Looked like it might have been one of the dead fellow's paintings to me."

"Great heavens, surely not!" Elizabeth shook her head. "I can't believe Violet was actually down here helping Sadie clean the cottage. No wonder she finished so promptly. I must say I'm quite flabbergasted. Violet does pitch in now and again when things get desperate, but I can't imagine why she felt it necessary to help Sadie with the cottage. After all, it wasn't exactly an emergency. Though I suppose Violet might have felt it was one, since we do want to rent the cottage again."

She'd been more or less talking to herself, and was quite taken aback when Captain Carbunkle said firmly, "Ho, but they didn't clean the cottage, your ladyship. No sir. They walked in, stayed a few minutes, then came on out again. Couldn't have got much cleaning done in that time, I'm thinking."

"Yes," Elizabeth murmured, "I'm afraid you're right. I'll have to have a word with them when I get back. I must say, Captain, you've been remarkably observant."

The captain tucked his thumbs under the lapels of his navy blue reefer jacket. "Pride myself on that, Lady Elizabeth. Not much goes on around here that I don't notice. Comes from years of staring out to sea, watching for signs of land. You notice the slightest little thing out of place. Gets to be a habit in the end."

"Quite." Elizabeth pulled on her glove and grasped the handlebars of her motorcycle. "I also heard that spending many years at sea makes one a light sleeper."

Captain Carbunkle shrugged. "Can't speak for everyone, of course, but I will say the least sound can wake me up. If it's not what I'm used to hearing, that is."

"Of course." Elizabeth carefully lifted a leg across the saddle and seated herself. "Then perhaps you heard or saw something out of place early yesterday morning?"

For a moment it seemed as though the captain had not understood her question. He stared blankly at her, then managed to get out a few stumbling words. "Yesterday morning? What, here? Oh, well, no . . . I didn't . . . that is . . ."

Elizabeth paused in the act of straightening her skirt. "It's quite all right, Wally. I'm not accusing you of anything. I just wondered if perhaps you'd heard or seen something that might help in the investigation of the murder." She saw no point in informing the captain that as far as the local constabulary was concerned, there *was* no investigation.

"No, your . . . m'm . . . no, I wouldn't have seen anything because . . ." His voice trailed off, even though his mouth continued to open and close.

Regarding his deeply flushed face, Elizabeth became quite concerned. The captain's confusion was obvious. The man seemed to be having trouble voicing words, and his gaze darted about in every direction except at her. "Because what, Captain?" she prompted gently.

"Because . . . because . . ." His final words came out in a rush. "I wasn't here that night. I was . . . out of town. Yes, that's it. Out of town. Had some business to take care of in North Horsham. Didn't get back until last night."

"I see." Elizabeth stared at him thoughtfully. "Well, I won't keep you any longer, Captain."

Captain Carbunkle looked vastly relieved as he lifted his cap from his head. "Good day, your ladyship. Don't forget to let me know if there's anything I can do."

Short of finding a new tenant for the cottage, there wasn't much he could do, Elizabeth thought as she roared off down the lane. Unless he could explain to her just why he was so agitated when she'd asked him if he'd heard anything the morning of the murder. Now that was something for which she'd really like an answer.

CHAPTER

❀ 7 ❀

It wasn't often that the lady of the manor visited the tiny hairdresser's shop in the High Street. Heads turned in surprise and all chattering ceased when Elizabeth walked in that morning. Unfazed by all the attention, she gave the two waiting customers a cordial greeting then headed for the end basin, where Marlene was busy rinsing another customer's tresses.

"I wonder if you could spare the time to have a word with me," she announced when Marlene stared wide-eyed at her. "I won't keep you long."

Marlene looked down at her customer, whose head was half-buried facedown in the basin. "Well, I'm in the middle of doing Mrs. Crumm's hair right now, your ladyship."

A mumbling sound came from the wet head in the basin.

Elizabeth puffed out her breath. Just her luck to run into Rita Crumm. She really wasn't in the mood for a battle of wits with the cantankerous woman. Rita's efforts to outshine her at every conceivable opportunity had become extremely tiresome.

True, the woman did her part for the war effort, with the help of her infamous Housewives League. Her sometimes misplaced enthusiasm was legendary, as was her undying and most certainly mistaken belief that she would eventually be awarded the Order of the British Empire for her endeavors.

There was no denying that Rita was a born organizer and her knitting, sewing, collecting, and money-raising committees had produced a wealth of products. It was her attitude Elizabeth found so infuriating. The woman simply could not tolerate the fact that Elizabeth's mother had been nothing more than a kitchen maid when she'd married the Earl of Wellsborough. In Rita's biased opinion, Elizabeth did not deserve the title of lady of the manor, and she rarely missed an opportunity to display her disapproval.

Right now, however, she was at a distinct disadvantage, being half drowned by the stream of water Marlene was pouring over her head.

Enjoying the rare moment, Elizabeth raised her voice to overpower the agitated woman's sputtered protests. "That's quite all right, Marlene. I shall take a seat in the foyer and read one of those interesting little film magazines while I wait. Just take your time."

Marlene grabbed a towel and wrapped it around Rita's head. "I'll be with you in a tick, your ladyship."

Elizabeth moved away, thankfully out of earshot, as

Rita emerged from the basin. In the foyer she took a seat next to Marjorie Gunther, who immediately broke off her conversation with the woman next to her and beamed at the new arrival.

"Lovely to see you down here, Lady Elizabeth. Come to get your hair done, have you?"

"Not exactly," Elizabeth began, but Marge, as everyone called her, wasn't listening as usual.

"Couldn't find a better hairdresser than our Marlene, that's for sure. Got the most soothing fingers, she has."

"Yes, I—"

"Nothing more relaxing than getting your hair shampooed, that's what I say. You can just sit there and let your mind wander off wherever it will, don't you think?"

"Well, I—"

"We all need to relax in these dreadful times, don't we. Doesn't do to sit there worrying about things we can't do anything about, does it."

Elizabeth glanced at the lady next to Marge, who sat behind the pages of a magazine with an expression of relief. There were several more magazines lying on the table. Perhaps, if she simply picked one up, Marge would get the hint and stop chattering in her ear.

She reached out a hand just as Marge said, "I need something to relax me after what we saw on the cliffs yesterday morning."

Elizabeth pulled her hand back. "On the cliffs?"

Obviously delighted that her audience finally showed interest, Marge nodded her head. "Oh, yes, your ladyship. We were on our morning patrol. Every morning at half past seven, rain or shine. Never miss a day, we don't. You can bet if we did, that'd be the day the Jerries would decide to come and invade us. That's for sure. I was just saying to Rita, I was—"

"Yes, but what was it you saw on the cliffs?"

Marge looked a bit taken aback by this rather abrupt interruption, but instantly recovered. "Well, your ladyship, we saw this man standing on the cliffs. He was looking out to sea with them field glasses. Rita calls them binoc . . . something."

"Binoculars."

"That's right. Always knows the fancy words for things, does our Rita. She knows a lot of stuff like that. Clever old cow, she is. Reckon she swallowed a dictionary or something." Marge laughed heartily at her weak joke.

Elizabeth gritted her teeth. "So what was the man doing up there?"

Marge glanced around the shop as if afraid someone was going to pounce on her. "Well, m'm," she said, lowering her voice to a murmur, "that's just it, isn't it. He told Rita he was bird-watching. Likely story, that one. He didn't look like any bird-watcher I've ever seen. If you ask me, he looked more like a blinking German spy."

"Really." Elizabeth pursed her lips. "And what does a German spy look like?"

Marge seemed confused by the question. "Well, your ladyship, I suppose he . . . well, I really don't know . . . like a bird-watcher, maybe? I mean, what was he really watching through them glasses, that's what I want to know."

Elizabeth suppressed a stab of irritation. There was enough to worry about in wartime without suspecting the worst of every person who didn't conform to one's idea of normality. "Well, I really wouldn't worry about it. I'm sure if he were a spy, he wouldn't be that obvious. He was more than likely watching birds, just as he said."

Obviously disappointed, Marge slumped down in her

chair. "I s'pose so. But he was acting really strange. Said he was staying at the Tudor Arms, but when Rita left him, he walked off in the other direction."

Elizabeth was saved from answering by Marlene's soft voice at her shoulder. "Your ladyship? I can spare a few minutes now. Sorry to keep you waiting. Would you like to come into the back room? I can make you a nice cup of tea."

Elizabeth rose with a smile. "The back room will do very well. Thank you, Marlene."

She followed the girl through the faded blue-striped curtain that shielded the back room from prying eyes. Actually, the room was little bigger than a cupboard, but it had a couple of armchairs and a gas ring for boiling water.

The cubby hole afforded scant privacy, but the loud hum of a hair dryer obscured the conversation. Elizabeth settled herself on one of the chairs and declined the offer of tea. "I really can't stay that long," she said as Marlene sat down in the other chair. "Violet will be expecting me back for lunch quite soon."

Marlene nodded, a look of wary anticipation on her face. "I hope there's nothing wrong with Polly," she began, and Elizabeth hurried to reassure her.

"This has nothing to do with your sister. I know this is none of my business, but I was wondering if you could tell me about the man who almost ran you down yesterday morning."

Marlene's eyes widened in surprise. "Pete? Why? What's he been up to?"

"Nothing as far as I know. I was merely wondering what his business in town might be." Aware that she was treading on delicate ground, Elizabeth sought for a feasible excuse. Remembering the letter she'd read that morning gave her one. "There have been some rumors about a new factory being built nearby, and I was wondering if this man has anything to do with that."

Marlene seemed relieved. "Oh, no, m'm, I don't think so. I heard the rumors, too. In fact, Pete was telling me about this bloke what's staying at the Tudor Arms in the room next to him. Pete heard him asking the new barmaid about farmland around here. Doug Mc . . . something or other, his name was. 'Course, the barmaid didn't know nothing, since she hasn't been here that long, neither. Pete told him to ask at the town hall."

Surprised to hear the rumors apparently being borne out, Elizabeth asked, "Did he say why he was looking for the land?"

"Not as far as I know, m'm. At least Pete didn't say so. I wouldn't be surprised if the chap's looking for somewhere to build the factory, though. I wouldn't mind getting a job there if they build one close enough. Make more money than washing hair, and I'd be doing me bit for the war effort. They've been on to me about that already."

Assuming that "they" meant the War Office, Elizabeth murmured, "I suppose we all have to do our bit."

"Well, you're doing yours, all right, your ladyship, having them Yanks billeted at the Manor House. Must be a lot of work. Polly said she's glad she doesn't have to do the housework anymore. Though Sadie seems to like it well enough."

Aware that they were getting away from the topic, Elizabeth said smoothly, "Things seem to be working out very well at the manor. I'm not so sure we want a factory built that close to us, though. That could make us a target for enemy bombs."

Marlene's face whitened. "Oh, gawd, your ladyship. I never thought of that."

"Well, we mustn't jump to conclusions until we know

more about it. You're quite sure that this young man you're seeing has nothing to do with the factory?"

Marlene thought about it, then shrugged. "To be perfectly honest, m'm, I don't really know what he's doing down here. He likes to ask lots of questions—I do know that. He says he lives in Surrey, but when I asked him why he came down to Sitting Marsh, he joked around and never told me nothing. I do know he's got money . . . I mean he drives a really posh car and wears nice clothes and he wears a gold watch and talks posh and everything. But he doesn't like to talk about himself." She stared down at her hands and twisted her fingers together. After a moment, she looked up with a worried frown marring her pretty face. "He seems really nice, though, m'm. I really don't think he means no harm."

Elizabeth patted her hand. "I'm sure he doesn't, dear. I was just curious, that's all. If he should tell you anything you think I should know, you will tell me, won't you?"

Marlene nodded earnestly. "Of course I will, m'm." She jumped as a bell rang somewhere in the shop. "Oops! Gotta get Mrs. Crumm out from under the dryer. She'll give me heck if I don't get out there."

"Then by all means, we mustn't keep her waiting." Elizabeth rose from the chair. "This man who was asking about farmland . . . his name is Doug, you say?"

"Yes, m'm. McNeil or MacNamara . . . something like that. The barmaid will tell you. She seems to be getting things going down at the Tudor Arms. Pete says all the rooms are full, and the bars are crowded every night."

"Then I must certainly pay them a visit." Elizabeth gathered up her handbag and gloves. "Thank you, Marlene, and I hope your friendship with the young man continues to flourish."

"Thank you, m'm. I hope so, too. He's really nice."

Marlene's wistful expression as she led the way from the back room gave Elizabeth cause to doubt the outcome of that relationship. She felt rather sorry for the girl. For all the single women in the village, come to that. What with all the young men in the village away fighting, leaving only the servicemen in the area for company, any hopes of a serious bond seemed unlikely.

She had no idea why a vision of Major Monroe should flit through her mind on the heels of that thought. Or if she did, she deliberately squashed the notion. There could be no serious bond for her . . . even if Earl Monroe's marriage wasn't all it should be. And she had no right to feel that little lift in her heart at the reminder of his disturbing words.

The best thing she could do for everyone concerned was get herself down to the Tudor Arms, and she would do so right after lunch, before they closed for the afternoon. Perhaps the new barmaid would tell her more about Peter Weston, and while she was about it, this Doug person as well. It wouldn't hurt to find out more about the bird-watcher on the cliffs either, since it appeared that Peter Weston wasn't the only one in the vicinity of Sandhill Lane in the early hours of yesterday morning.

Polly slipped the last invoice into the file marked XYZ, then carefully closed the drawer. The file cabinet was actually an antique dresser from the bedroom of Lord and Lady Wellsborough. Polly had been given strict orders to treat it with gentle loving care. She didn't always pay heed to the request. Especially when she was in a hurry. Today, however, she'd finished the filing in record time and still had almost an hour before lunch would be served.

Might as well go and help Sadie, she told herself as she pulled open the door. It would give her another excuse to hang around the east wing. Not that she had much hope of seeing Sam again. He was more than likely at the base. How she hated it when he was gone. She never knew if he was flying over Germany and getting shot at. Still, with all the storms they'd had lately, there hadn't been many missions going out.

She glanced out the windows of the great hall while she walked down to the east wing. The branches of the massive elms were tossing around, waving their arms as if they were mad at each other. The raindrops had started again, and chased each other down the narrow window panes. A cold draft brought out goosebumps on her arms, and she rubbed them as she hurried down the thick carpeted hallway.

She was almost at the bathroom when she saw the tall figure stride around the corner. At first she thought her longing for him had dreamed him up in her mind, but then he marched toward her and her heart leapt. "Sam!" Forgetting all the tension between them, she flew up to him, her arms outstretched to throw around him.

She was inches away when he held up his hands and stepped back, away from her. She came to an abrupt halt, feeling as if he'd poured cold water on her head. The hard look on his poor, scarred face was enough to bring tears to her eyes.

"Hello, Sam," she said, striving to keep the tremble out of her voice. "It's good to see you again."

He barely moved his lips when he answered her. "I was just on my way out."

"Going to the base?"

"Yep." He walked past her, heading for the stairs.

Desperate for one tiny spark of encouragement, she called out his name.

He paused, but kept his back to her.

"I was just wondering if you'd been down to the pub since the new barmaid started working there," she said, her heart thumping so fiercely she could barely get out the words. "It's really lively down there now. They have a song night on Sundays and everything."

"I don't go to the pub anymore. I haven't been down there in weeks."

The bitterness in his voice made her cringe. "Well, I was just thinking, if you wanted to go down there—"

"Polly!" His harsh voice made her jump, cutting off her words. "Give it up, will you?"

Close to tears now, she said brokenly, "I'll never give it up, Sam. I'll never stop loving you. Never. One day you'll realize that no one is going to love you as much as I do. No matter if I never see you again as long as I live, I'll never love no one else. Never."

"Polly . . ."

His voice was softer now, and a tiny ray of hope began to burn. She waited, holding her breath, but after an agonizing moment or two of silence, he shook his head and stalked off toward the stairs. She waited until he was out of sight, then ran back to the study, her eyes misted with tears.

Sadie whistled loudly as she trudged down the vast hallway a little later. Her buckets swung in each hand so hard the tins of polish rattled against the bottle of bleach. She liked to make lots of noise while she was alone in the great hall.

There was something creepy about the long expanse of walls with all them pictures of dead people hanging on them. Not one of them smiling, neither. 'Course, if she had to dress up in all them ruffles and corsets and stiff collars, she wouldn't be smiling, neither.

Sadie paused at the first window and put down her buckets. Peering through the rain-smeared glass, she frowned at the tossing trees. Never seen such weather like it, she hadn't. Didn't rain like this in London. Nor blow like that, neither. Couldn't hardly keep a brolly up in that wind.

She could just see all them London toffs scurrying along the Strand holding their bowler hats with one hand and clinging to umbrellas turned inside out by the wind. The vision made her giggle, and she turned back to her buckets, then paused when she saw Martin standing by the suit of armor at the far end of the great hall.

Ever since she'd started working at the manor, Martin had treated her like she was dirt beneath his shoes. Stuffy old bugger wouldn't even crack a smile when she joked with him.

Sadie wasn't used to people ignoring her. No matter how miserable someone was, she usually managed to get a grin out of them sooner or later.

It was Sadie's firm belief that the whole world would be a happier place and there'd be no more wars if everyone smiled every minute of every day. Once she'd even made a guard outside Buckingham Palace twitch his mouth. Weren't many people who could do that. But Martin remained a lost cause, no matter what she said or did. Didn't mean she was going to give up on him, though. The old codger could do with a good belly laugh now and then.

Squaring her shoulders, Sadie took a firm grip on the handles of her buckets and marched with grim determination toward Martin's bowed figure.

She was almost up to him before he saw her. He had his hand outstretched toward the suit of armor, as if he was about to lift the visor on the helmet. When he realized she was bearing down on him, he snatched his hand back and pushed it in his trouser pocket.

She reached him, and dropped her buckets on the floor with a loud rattle, making him wince. "Hello, me old mate," she said with a lusty wink. "Watcha up to, then?"

Martin got that look in his eye as if he'd tasted something bad. "My name, in case you have forgotten, is Martin. If you must address me at all, kindly refer to me by my proper name."

His lips sort of pinched together, making Sadie grin. "Oo, proper snotty this morning, ain't we. What's the matter, duck? Got out the wrong side of the bed, did we?"

Martin's chin raised several inches—a miracle considering how scrunched up his body was. "My bedroom habits are none of your business, missy. So get on with your work and cease pestering me, unless you want me to report you to madam for slovenly behavior."

"Slovenly." Sadie slowly rolled the word around her tongue. "What a posh word! What kind of behavior would that be then, duck?"

Martin blinked, and glared at her over the top of his gold-rimmed glasses. "I am not a duck. I am a butler and your superior. I am not obliged to stand here and listen to your impertinent drivel."

"Quite right, Marty, me old mate. Standing still will make your bones creak. Why don't we dance? Here"— she held out her arms—"how about a fling around the great hall? I bet you could show me a thing or two."

Martin's look of horror almost choked her. "I shall report your despicable behavior to madam. If I were you, I'd start packing my bags immediately."

Sadie picked up her buckets. "Suit yourself, but you're missing a real treat. I was just trying to jolly you up a bit, that's all. You look as if you could use a laugh or two.

Nobody likes to stare at a miserable face all day long. It wouldn't hurt you to smile now and then."

Martin looked offended. "Not that I have to answer to you, but I'd like you to know that I'm perfectly capable of seeing humor in a situation in the proper place at the proper time. And with the proper people."

Sadie sighed. "Meaning I'm not proper, is that it? Well, all I can say is that if being proper means going about with a face that looks as if it would crack if it smiled, I'd rather not be proper, thank you."

"I see no fear of that miracle ever coming to pass," Martin said, turning his back on her.

Sadie shook her head then, giving up the battle, trudged toward the stairs. She paused at the top of them and looked back over her shoulder. Martin was still hovering around the suit of armor, patting it here and there as if he was looking for something. Intrigued in spite of herself, she watched him for a moment or two.

He stood there for the longest time, staring up at the helmet, and seemed to be muttering to himself. She couldn't hear what he said, but it was almost as if he was talking to the armor. She'd done that herself on more than one occasion, but in a joking way. This was different. It gave her the willies to see the old man talking so earnestly to an empty pile of metal. Like he was talking to a real person.

A shiver chased down her back, and she turned and ran down the stairs. What with the cottage in Sandhill Lane and the crazy bugger in the great hall of the manor, it was a wonder she didn't go white overnight. There was a lot of creepy stuff going on, and not for the first time, she wondered if perhaps she hadn't made a mistake moving down from London. Right then she couldn't decide what was worse . . . Hitler's bombs or the gremlins of Sitting Marsh.

CHAPTER

❦ 8 ❦

It was much later that day before Elizabeth found the time to slip down to the Tudor Arms. When she'd arrived back at the manor earlier for lunch, she was met with a contingent of anxious tenants voicing their concerns about the possibility of a new factory being built close to the village.

By the time she'd convinced them that no one would build a factory without the approval of the town council, lunch had been delayed at least an hour, much to Violet's disgust.

"This is our main meal of the day," she complained as Elizabeth joined Martin, Sadie, and Polly at the spacious kitchen table. "The only one we all take together. Short of a disaster, nothing should be allowed to interfere with it."

"If you ask me," Martin observed, "this daily ritual has become something of a disaster. If I may be permitted to say so, and as I have expressed many times, madam should not be partaking in meals served at the kitchen table in the company of the downstairs staff. It is unheard of, most improper, and the master is highly displeased."

"The master is dead and gone, Martin." Violet raised her eyebrows at Elizabeth. "Which is a blessing if you ask me. If he were alive, he'd find a lot more than madam's eating habits to complain about."

Ignoring the barb, Elizabeth unfolded her serviette. "It's my business where I choose to dine. Sitting at that enormous table on my own in that drafty dining room is far too miserable for comfort. I much prefer the warmth and companionship of the kitchen. Bearing the duties of the lady of the manor should at least entitle me to dine where I please."

"But not when," Violet said tartly. "You can't expect me to keep everything warm without cremating it. Look at these mashed potatoes. They look like curbside snow after motorcars and bikes have been sloshing through it."

"They always look like that," Martin commented. "What's more, they taste like it, as well."

"How would you know, you silly old goat," Violet muttered. "You lost your sense of taste with your teeth half a century ago."

Polly giggled, while Sadie gave Martin a broad wink. "Don't you take no notice of her, Marty, me old mate. You do all right for a hundred-year-old gentleman."

Martin's nose twitched, sending his glasses even lower. "If you continue to insult me, young lady, I can promise you a much shorter lifetime than that." He raised his hand to rescue his glasses before they slipped right off his nose. As he did so, the cuff of his sleeve flapped open, slapping him smartly on the chin.

"Martin!" Violet's exclamation of outrage made them all jump. "Where are your cufflinks? You forgot to put them in again, didn't you."

Martin tucked both his hands beneath the edge of the table, hiding them from view. "I did not forget," he said in an injured tone. "I simply mislaid them, that's all."

"What do you mean you mislaid them? They have to be in your room somewhere. They wouldn't just fall out."

"I'd have seen them if they had," Sadie said, earning a glare from Violet for her trouble.

"I can't believe it." Violet shook her head in obvious dismay. "First your pocket watch, now your cufflinks. What are you doing with your things? Selling them?"

"Of course not." Martin folded the cuffs of his sleeves back—something Elizabeth had never seen him do in her life. "Why do you have to make such a fuss about everything, Violet? I've simply misplaced the pesky things, that's all. I'll come across them, no doubt."

"Well, you can't have lost all your cufflinks. Why didn't you put some other ones in?"

Martin looked defiant. "Because I chose not to, that's why. Kindly refrain from treating me like a child."

"I will if you stop acting like one."

Deciding it was time to intervene, Elizabeth said hurriedly, "I happened to pass by the cottage in Sandhill Lane this morning, Violet. Captain Carbunkle mentioned that you had helped Sadie clean the cottage."

Violet dumped a steaming bowl of vegetables on the table. "The girl was too scared to go down there by herself."

"I wasn't scared," Sadie protested. "I just don't like messing about with the devil, that's all."

Polly uttered a small gasp. "What devil?"

"Oh, take no notice of her. She's just being a silly twerp." Violet placed a large platter of fat brown sausages next to the vegetables.

The aroma of fried sausage and onions tended to make Elizabeth's mouth water. Hoping to speed things up a bit, she murmured, "Well, it was very nice of you to help Sadie, Violet. I'm sure she appreciates it."

"Oh, I do, m'm," Sadie assured her. "Except we didn't have to do no cleaning. It was all done when we got there." She lowered her voice to a chilling whisper. "By invisible hands. Like I said, the devil's work."

Polly's face turned pale. "Go on! Really?"

"No, not really," Violet said crossly. "Someone cleaned up the place, all right, but it wasn't no devil's doing. He wouldn't have been that tidy." She glanced at Elizabeth. "Must have been the investigators."

"No doubt," Elizabeth murmured, wondering what kind of criminal investigator would go to all that trouble to clean up after himself.

"Well, all I can say," Sadie announced as Violet placed a large tureen of brown gravy on the table, "is that bringing that picture back from there is asking for trouble."

Violet straightened her back and cuffed Sadie smartly behind the ear. "You're the one asking for trouble, my girl. It's none of your business what I do."

"Ow!" Sadie rubbed her ear, and glowered at Violet, but wisely kept a still tongue.

Martin wasn't quite as prudent. "It's about time someone taught that young hussy a lesson," he muttered.

"That's enough out of you, too."

Violet lifted her hand, and for a startling moment, Elizabeth thought she might bat at Martin, too. "What picture is that?" Elizabeth asked loudly.

"It's one of Mr. Thorncroft's paintings." Violet sat down, still wearing her pained expression. "I put it in your study. It was in the dustbin with a bunch of others. It's a shame to waste a good painting. I think it was the one you saw on the easel. I thought it would look nice on the wall. Since no one seems to want it, I saw no harm in bringing it home."

"I suppose not," Elizabeth said doubtfully. "If anyone asks for it, we can always give it back."

"No one's going to ask for it." Violet shook out her serviette. "The dustmen will be around tomorrow to pick up the rubbish, and then they'll all be gone."

"In that case, thank you, Violet. I shall enjoy the painting."

"Are we going to say grace, madam?" Martin looked a trifle irritated. "The aroma of those sausages is making me quite ravenous."

"Of course, Martin." Elizabeth recited grace, anxious now to finish her meal. She was looking forward to hanging the new painting in her study and couldn't wait to get up there to take a good look at it. It had been so long since she'd had anything new for her office.

Deciding that her visit to the Tudor Arms would have to wait until opening time that evening, she slipped away from the kitchen at the first opportunity and headed for the study. Polly, having finished her work up there, had volunteered to help Sadie, who had fallen behind in her schedule.

Elizabeth was pleased that the girls seemed to be getting along so well together. They were both strong-willed, and she'd been concerned that they might squabble. So far that hadn't happened. After all, a happy household made it so much more pleasant for everyone. Now, if only Violet and Martin could see eye to eye, the atmosphere in the manor would be relatively peaceful.

Alone in her office at last, Elizabeth picked up the painting that Violet had left standing against her desk. It really was a most attractive picture, and she was anxious to see how it looked on the wall. But first, she had to decide which wall it should go on.

She carried it over to the window to study how the light would play on the canvas. As she held it up, something struck her as familiar about the building in the foreground. It looked a lot like the Tudor Arms. Except it couldn't be.

Frowning, Elizabeth laid the painting flat on her desk and leaned over it. Yes, it most certainly was the pub. The narrow latticed windows, the sloping roof, the dark crossbeams, and the rickety fence bordering the car park were all there. If that wasn't enough, a small square blob was obviously the sign that hung from the post outside. There was even a smudged figure standing in front of the door with a hand raised above the head, though the image was too indistinct to recognize. The person, whoever it was, appeared to be waving at the artist.

Nevertheless, there was something definitely odd about the scene. Although Elizabeth could easily recognize the sweep of the bay beyond the coast road, and the bushy trees that edged the woods—even the rows of tiny cottages that nestled on the slopes of the downs had been faithfully depicted, as well as the shadowy outline of the Manor House on the hill—the Tudor Arms, if it was indeed that ancient and distinctive building, was in the wrong place.

The pub didn't belong on the edge of the cliffs as it appeared in the painting. It was farther down the hill, away from the shoreline, and would have been out of sight at that angle.

Somewhat let down by this inaccuracy, Elizabeth chided herself. Basil Thorncroft no doubt wanted the picturesque pub in his picture, and since it couldn't be seen from a spot that had obviously pleased him enough to use for his scene, he had simply inserted the historic building, taking artistic license. Which he certainly had the right to do.

Nevertheless, it took the edge off her pleasure of the picture, and she leaned it against the wall, intending to decide later where she wanted to hang it. Right now, she had more important things to take care of, and if she wanted to talk to the new barmaid before the pub got too busy, she would have to leave soon. The painting would just have to wait.

"I tell you I saw him," Sadie said as she emptied the bucket of dirty water outside the back door of the kitchen. "He was talking to the suit of armor, and patting it, like he was looking for something. Barmy, he is. Nutty as a fruitcake."

"It's not your place to talk about Martin like that. He might be a little fuzzy about some things, but he's still of sound mind." Violet slammed a cupboard door shut a little harder than necessary. "After all, we all talk to ourselves at times. Even you. I'm sure Martin had a perfectly good reason for addressing the armor. More than likely he was noticing the dust. There are some people who can't see dust an inch thick."

" 'Ere," Sadie exclaimed. "I hope you're not talking about me. I never leave a speck of dust anywhere. You can go and look for yourself."

Violet, aware that her irritation was largely due to her

concerns about Martin, felt compelled to give the girl her due. "Did I mention any names? I never said I was talking about you. Anyway, get off with you and finish your jobs, or you'll be staying late tonight instead of gadding about down the pub with the Americans."

Sadie opened the pantry door and shoved the bucket under a shelf. "I don't waste me time gadding about with the Yanks. Too many women to fight off. No man's worth fighting over, that's what I say."

"You seem to spend enough time down there." Violet took a pencil and pad out of a drawer and sat down with them at the kitchen table.

"I like playing darts with the blokes." Sadie crossed the floor to the sink and started filling it with hot water. "You learn a lot that way."

Violet sniffed. "The only thing you learn in a place like that is you're better off not being there."

"You learn a lot more than that." Sadie dumped the dinner plates into the foaming water. "Like this German spy what's supposed to be hiding in the village."

Violet paused in the act of scribbling out her shopping list. "A spy? Who told you that?"

"The rozzers . . . constables. I thought everyone knew about it by now. Ethel Goffin, you know . . . Sid's wife? Well, she told Marlene while she was doing her hair, and Marlene told Polly, and Polly told me. It was supposed to be a secret, but everybody's talking about it. It was all over the pub last night."

Violet clicked her tongue. "That Sid Goffin never did know how to keep his mouth shut. Talk about loose lips sinking ships. If it was up to him, he'd sink the whole blinking country. How he stayed in the police force all them years I'll never know."

"I s'pose it's natural you want to tell your wife. It was

her fault for blabbing it out in the hairdresser's." Sadie stopped washing dishes and got a faraway look in her eye. "It's nice he told her, though. I'd want my husband to tell me everything."

Violet snorted. "Men should know how to keep their traps shut."

"Well, all I hope is that they catch the bugger before he finds any secrets. Polly says he's after secret papers at the American base."

"Not so secret if Polly knows about them."

"She don't know about the papers, just that he's after them."

"Well, if you ask me, it's all a bunch of horse manure. The way rumors get started in this town makes my head spin."

"Well, I heard that the ladies in the Housewives League actually saw him."

Thoroughly startled by this unexpected news, Violet dropped her pencil. "The spy? Where?"

Sadie abandoned the dishes and came over to sit down at the table. "On the cliffs. One of them told Marlene that they were all walking out there yesterday morning and saw this bloke looking out to sea through a pair of field glasses. He said he was a bird-watcher. They don't think he was no bird watcher. They think he was the spy. After what Sid's wife told Marlene, they put two and two together."

"And came up with seven as usual." Determined not to let on to the girl how worried she was, Violet picked up her pencil again. "All this nonsense about spies running around Sitting Marsh. Whatever next. Get on with the dishes, for heaven's sake, and let me finish this shopping list."

"Well, just don't tell Polly I told you. Like I said, it's

supposed to be a secret." Sadie got up from her chair and went back to the sink. "Though, if you ask me, if there really is a spy, the more people what know about it the better. That way we can all keep a lookout for him."

"And accuse everyone who looks a little bit funny," Violet muttered. "Fat lot of good that'll do."

"It might help catch the bugger." Sadie held up a plate and let the soapsuds drip from it before standing it in the rack to dry. "Otherwise he could tell them Jerries to come and bomb the base. Right pickle we'd be in then."

Violet suppressed a cold stab of fear. "Stop talking nonsense and finish them dishes. I want to see them all dried and put away when I come back."

Sadie twisted her head around to look at her. "Why? Where are you going?"

"Never you mind. I'll be back before you know it, so get cracking." Violet hurried from the room, Sadie's words echoing like sharp icicles in her heart. Surely, *surely,* it couldn't be true? The girl had to be repeating harmless rumors, that's all. There was always some rumor going around about invasions and air raids and German pilots landing by parachute. None of them turned out to be true. Except for the parachute bit. Still, this was the first time she'd ever heard talk of a spy. It wouldn't hurt to have a word with Polly when she saw her.

Right now, however, she had something else on her mind. It wasn't like Martin to lose his things. First the pocket watch and now the cufflinks. Martin didn't have a lot of worldly belongings, but those he did have were quite valuable, mostly given to him by the master over the years.

Both the watch and the cufflinks would fetch a good price anywhere. Except that she knew full well that Martin put a tremendous amount of stock in sentimental value,

and would never willingly part with his treasured posses-
sions. At least, he wouldn't as long as he was thinking
straight.

Sadie's talk of Martin holding a conversation with the
suit of armor made her nervous. It wouldn't hurt to take
a look in his room, providing he wasn't in it, of course.
If he had simply mislaid the things, as he said he had,
they shouldn't be too hard to find. She could just slip them
back where they belonged and he'd never be any the
wiser.

Reaching the door of his room, she tapped on it, ready
with an excuse if he should open it. When the door remained closed for several seconds, she carefully turned
the handle and peeked inside. "Martin?" she called out.
"You in there?"

The silence encouraged her, and she slipped inside the
room and closed the door. In spite of his age, Martin kept
his quarters immaculate. Polly, or rather Sadie now, was
allowed in only once a week to clean, and that under his
close supervision. Violet felt uneasy about being in there
without his approval, but when a problem became urgent,
one had to do what one thought best under the circumstances.

Moving over to the small bedside table, Violet carefully
opened a drawer and peered inside. A small Bible lay
nestled next to a neat layer of socks, all carefully folded.
White handkerchiefs were piled next to them and, in the
corner, a black velvet-covered box.

Violet opened the box, expecting to see an array of
cufflinks and tie pins. There was only one pair of links—
tarnished silver—obviously very old. Martin had at least
three pairs of expensive gold links, as far as Violet was
aware. Probably more. Where they were was a mystery.

A quick search of the dresser drawers produced no sign

of the missing jewelry, or the pocket watch. In the bottom drawer of the dresser, however, she lifted up two pairs of pajamas and underneath discovered something quite unforeseen. A delicate white lace handkerchief.

Holding it to her nose, Violet sniffed. Eau de cologne, without a doubt. Frowning, she slipped it back in its place and closed the drawer. Now, where in the world did Martin come into possession of a lady's handkerchief? It had to be recently, since the fragrance was still detectable.

With a little huff of exasperation, she headed for the door. Just as she reached it, something else caught her attention. Martin's carved whalebone, given to him by his grandfather, usually hung on the wall above his bed. The piece was priceless, and Martin's most valued possession. He'd told Violet once, in a rare mood of confidence, that he felt his grandfather's presence whenever he looked at it, and never fell asleep without saying good night to it. Now, instead of the whalebone hanging from its gold cord, there was only an empty space.

Convinced now that something very strange was going on, Violet vowed to get to the bottom of it. Even if it meant upsetting the old goat.

She was about to return to the kitchen when she heard the clang of the front doorbell. She waited for a moment or two, but neither Sadie nor Martin seemed to be in the vicinity. Sighing loudly, she trudged up the stairs to the main hallway.

When she opened the door, the woman outside took a nervous step backward. "Oh," she said, "I was calling on Martin. Is he there?"

Recognizing Beatrice Carr, the lady with the raffle tickets, Violet narrowed her eyes. "He's indisposed at the moment," she said sharply.

"Oh, I see." The woman hovered for a moment or two,

as if she was considering full flight. Then she appeared to gather courage. "When would be a good time to call on him, then?"

"There's no telling. Sometimes he's around, sometimes he isn't."

Beatrice gazed up at her with anxious eyes. "He's not ill, is he?"

"Not as far as I know." Beginning to relent a little, Violet added grudgingly, "I'll tell him you were here. Perhaps next time he'll answer the door himself."

Beatrice nodded. "I certainly hope so. He is so generous. He's been buying so many raffle tickets. I'd really like to see him win something." She looked hopefully at Violet. "I don't suppose . . . ?"

"Not me. I don't believe in gambling. Thank you and goodbye." Violet closed the door, giving the woman no chance to reply. Raffle tickets, indeed. She didn't like that woman at all. It was time she had a good long talk with Martin.

CHAPTER
❦ 9 ❦

There were only a handful of customers in the lounge bar when Elizabeth arrived at the Tudor Arms shortly after opening time.

Alfie greeted her with his customary smile and a glass of her favorite sherry. "Nice to see you again, your ladyship. Don't see you down here that often."

Elizabeth hooked her hip over the edge of a barstool. "Thank you, Alfie. Much as I appreciate your hospitality, I'm afraid that an evening in the pub is not exactly my kind of entertainment."

Alfie nodded. "I can understand that, m'm. Too noisy, right?"

Elizabeth smiled. "Something like that. I understand the

noise level has increased somewhat since you've acquired an assistant."

Alfie swiped at the counter with a bright yellow cloth. "Oh, you mean Bridget? Yeah, she's bringing in a lot of new customers. Used to be dead as a doornail down here on Sundays. But she started a song night at the piano and word's been getting around. The place is packed on a Sunday night now."

"Oh, my, it sounds as if you have found a gem. I'd like to meet her."

Alfie glanced up at the clock on the wall. "She'll be here soon. Gets down here sharp at six. She's staying here at the pub for the time being."

Elizabeth took a quick sip of her sherry. "Is she looking for a place to rent, by any chance? The cottage in Sandhill Lane is ready to be occupied if she's interested."

Alfie's expression sobered. "Nasty business that. Got everyone nervous, it has. I'll be glad when they catch the bastard . . . begging your pardon, your ladyship."

"Not at all, Alfie. I have to admit, it's very unsettling to know a murderer could be running around the village. Did you know Mr. Thorncroft well?"

"He came in here a few times. Nice bloke. Didn't have much to say but always had a good word when he did." Alfie jerked his thumb at the ceiling. "He had his eye on Bridget . . . always giving her compliments, if you know what I mean. She liked it, as well. I could tell. She was really cut up when she heard about what happened to him."

"Oh, I'm so sorry. Then in that case, she probably won't want to live in the cottage."

"Well, you never know, do you, m'm. I mean, it's hard to tell what a woman wants these days. If you're going to be around for a while, though, you can ask her yourself. Like I said, she should be here any minute."

Elizabeth slid more securely onto her high perch. "I think I'll do just that, Alfie."

The bartender glanced down the lengthy bar to where a lanky, thin-faced gentleman sat brooding over a whiskey glass. "On the other hand, if you're wanting to rent that cottage, you might want to talk to Mr. Whitton over there. He's staying here, too. Supposed to be studying birds or something. I don't know how long he's thinking of staying in the village, but he might like to rent the cottage for a while. Give you time to find someone permanent."

Bird-watcher. He had to be the man Marjorie Gunther was speaking about earlier. Elizabeth studied the man from the corner of her eye. He sat hunched at the very end of the bar, with no apparent interest in what was going on around him.

"I don't know," she said doubtfully, but Alfie was already hailing the man.

"Hey, Whitton! Come and meet the lady of the manor. She doesn't honor us with her presence very often."

Uncomfortable now, Elizabeth watched the man approach with obvious reluctance. Alfie performed a quick introduction, then moved off to serve some customers who had just arrived, leaving Elizabeth alone with the newcomer.

"I'm delighted to meet you, your ladyship," Alistair Whitton said, sounding anything but pleased.

Elizabeth graciously inclined her head. "Likewise, I'm sure. Alfie tells me you are a bird-watcher. How interesting!"

His sharp brown eyes narrowed beneath hooded lids. "You are interested in ornithology?"

"I do like birds, yes, though I must confess, I'm not an expert. What kind of birds are you studying?"

"All kinds, but at the moment, I'm particularly interested in the migration patterns of the marsh species."

Elizabeth raised her eyebrows. "Really? Isn't it rather late in the year for migration?"

Alistair Whitton's expression took on a shade of disdain. "Not at all, your ladyship. The Arctic skua stays in the area well into October, along with the Manx shearwater."

Having never heard of either bird, Elizabeth blinked. "Really. Do they follow boats, too, like the gulls?"

"Gulls?"

"Yes."

Elizabeth raised her glass and studied the bird-watcher over the rim of it. "I heard that you were on the cliffs yesterday morning, looking out to sea."

A rather odd gleam appeared in Alistair Whitton's eyes. "I see. Sitting Marsh obviously has a rather efficient grapevine, Lady Elizabeth."

"It does indeed, Mr. Whitton. I should warn you as a newcomer, that the cliffs can be quite dangerous if one gets too close to the edge. Natural erosion, you see. We lose several inches a year from our shoreline."

"So I've heard." He hunched his shoulders again, his face now a mask of indifference. "No need to waste your concern on me, your ladyship. I have to admit to a devastating fear of heights. I can't even climb three steps of a ladder without a severe case of vertigo. Were it not for the barbed wire, I would not have ventured within ten feet of the cliff edge."

Elizabeth nodded. "Very wise, Mr. Whitton." She turned her head as Alfie spoke at her elbow.

"Lady Elizabeth, I'd like you to meet Bridget Watkins. Bridget, her ladyship."

The buxom woman dipped in an awkward curtsey, intriguing Elizabeth no end. It was rare that women curtsied nowadays. Especially one who looked as if she could hold her own in a match with an all-in wrestler. "I've heard some very nice things about you, Bridget," she said. "My assistant has been singing your praises, and Alfie tells me you are largely responsible for increasing the patronage of the Tudor Arms. It's a pleasure to welcome you to the village."

"Thank you, m'm. Very nice of you, I must say." Bridget looked lost for words, and darted a glance at Alfie, who was already on his way back to serve some customers.

Alistair Whitton cleared his throat. "If you'll excuse me, your ladyship, I think I'll call it a night."

Bridget appeared even more uncomfortable as the man strode out of the bar. "I didn't mean to interrupt anything, your ladyship."

"You didn't," Elizabeth said cheerfully. "To be honest, his conversation about birds went a little over my head."

"Strange, that one, your ladyship." Bridget fidgeted with her hair, stabbing at it with blunt fingers. "Doesn't like talking to people. I don't know why he bothers to come down to the bar. As soon as people start coming in, he leaves."

The barmaid's speech sounded stilted, as if she were weighing each word before she spoke. Doing her best to put the woman at ease, Elizabeth said airily, "Polly tells me you have a full house down here this week."

"That's right, m'm. All rooms fully booked. I'm glad I got mine before they filled up."

"Alfie tells me you might be interested in renting a cottage."

"He did?" Bridget sent a puzzled look in Alfie's direction. "Not really, your ladyship. The rent's cheap enough here, and I like living over my place of business. Always did it when I worked in the city. Saves me walking home on me own at night. Especially with all the storms we've been having lately. Nothing worse than having to turn out in the rain after a hard night's work."

"Yes, I see what you mean. So you've moved down from the city? London?"

Bridget gave a sharp negative shake of her head. "Birmingham."

"Is that so? I'd never have known it from your accent."

"I wasn't there very long, m'm." Bridget pulled a handkerchief from the pocket of her apron and covered her nose with it before blasting a sneeze into it. "Couldn't wait to get out of there. These days you're better off living in the country."

"Most certainly." Elizabeth sighed. "Though not too many people would agree with you. We don't get too many permanent residents anymore. I really would like to rent my cottage, though. I don't suppose you know anyone who's looking for a nice place to live?"

Bridget shrugged. "I could ask around, I s'pose. Someone might be looking for a little cottage to rent."

"What about Peter Weston? I understand he's staying here for the time being?"

"Pete?" Bridget stabbed at her hair again, leaving several blazing red strands in disarray. "I didn't know he was planning on hanging around that long. He lives near London, m'm. I got the impression he was only here on a short visit."

Elizabeth did her best to seem indifferent. "Oh, really?

I was rather hoping to have a word with him. Is he here, by any chance?"

"No, m'm. He's not. He met up with one of the local girls yesterday. Reckon he's with her."

"Ah, yes. That would be Marlene. Her sister, Polly, is my assistant. So how long has Mr. Weston been staying here?"

Bridget paused for a moment before answering. "A little over a week." She took down a glass tankard from a hook above her head and studied it for another long moment. "He isn't in any trouble, is he?"

Elizabeth hastened to reassure her. "Oh, no, it was just that I'd heard rumors about someone wanting to build a factory near the village and I would very much like to talk to whoever is responsible. I thought that Mr. Weston might be that person."

Bridget seemed relieved. She hung that tankard back on its hook, saying, "Oh, is that it. Well, your ladyship, I don't really know why Pete's down here, but I suppose it could be to scout about for land. Though someone else was asking about land last Saturday. Doug McNally. He's got a room here, too. You might want to talk to him as well."

"That sounds like a good idea." Elizabeth drained her glass. "Is he here?"

Bridget cast a glance around the room. "I can't see him right now, your ladyship. He might not be down yet. Bit of a deep one, he is. Doesn't say much. What with him and the bird-watcher, it's just as well we get a room full of Yanks, or this place would be as quiet as a tomb."

Elizabeth slid off her stool. That was hard to imagine. The noise level in the bar had risen considerably, and she had to raise her voice to be heard above the strident twanging of the out-of-tune piano. "Well, I shall just have to catch Mr. Weston and Mr. McNally later, that's all. Perhaps one of them will want to rent the cottage." She paused, then deliberately added, "I still can't believe that Mr. Thorncroft is dead. Such a nice man, and a talented artist. I can't imagine why anyone would want to kill him."

Bridget's face seemed to wither up, and she pursed her lips. "I don't suppose the police know who did it?"

"Not yet, as far as I know." Elizabeth pulled on her gloves. "Actually it's all rather a mystery. There doesn't seem to be any reason for anyone to do such an awful thing. Nothing was taken from the cottage, and apparently Mr. Thorncroft knew hardly anyone in the village. He hadn't lived here very long."

"He didn't seem to be the kind of man who would make enemies." Bridget reached below the counter for a damp cloth and swept the counter with it. "Doesn't make sense, does it, your ladyship. You don't expect something like murder in a small village like this."

"No, indeed. I understand you knew Mr. Thorncroft quite well?"

Bridget avoided her gaze. "I wouldn't exactly say that. We talked a bit. Nice man. Bit of a romancer, but he meant well. Most people seemed to like him. He always had a good word to say."

"That's nice, especially since he was a heavy drinker. Some men can get very belligerent when they drink too much."

Bridget looked surprised. "Basil? Oh, he never drank that much. Not that I saw, anyway. Never more than a pint or two of bitter."

Elizabeth studied her for a moment. "You don't say. He must have been quite friendly with the customers. Mr. Whitton or Mr. McNally, for instance?"

Bridget looked uneasy. "I couldn't really say, your ladyship. I don't have much time to notice much of what's going on around me."

"What about Peter Weston? Did he spend any time with Mr. Thorncroft?"

Bridget's lips thinned. "I really couldn't say, m'm."

Aware that she'd overstepped the boundaries of casual curiosity, Elizabeth changed the subject. The last thing she wanted to do at this point was advertise her vested interest in the case. "Well, I'm sure it must have been a great shock for you to hear the news."

"Oh, it certainly was, m'm. I had gone into North Horsham that morning, so I didn't hear about it until I got back. I had to get some extra beer. We were getting short because of the song night the night before."

"Ah yes, everyone has been telling me about that. It sounds as if you all have a wonderful time."

"We do, indeed, m'm. Prissy plays the piano really well—"

"Prissy?"

"I think her name is Priscilla Pierce."

Elizabeth nodded, wondering how the prim and proper Priscilla liked being called Prissy.

"Then there's her boyfriend, Captain Carbunkle. He's got such a lovely voice. He entertained everybody this last Sunday. He was singing sea shanties that sailors used to sing on the old sailing ships. All the customers were on their feet clapping and cheering. It was quite a night."

Elizabeth stared at her. She wasn't sure what surprised her the most—to hear Wally described as Priscilla's boyfriend or that Wally had been in the pub that night. Just to make sure, she asked, "Captain Carbunkle was here on Sunday night?"

"Yes, m'm. He's here every Sunday night. I think he

comes down to be with Prissy, though he does love to sing."

Elizabeth frowned. "He was here all that evening?"

Bridget nodded. "Left just before closing time. He seemed in a hurry." She laughed, a hearty, rather caustic sound that rang out above the chatter. "Seeing as how taken he is with Prissy, I was surprised he'd left alone." She looked up at the clock. "Excuse me, your ladyship, but it's starting to get busy. I should be getting along . . ."

"Of course. I must be off myself." Elizabeth collected her thoughts. "I'm so happy that the Tudor Arms is in such good hands. Alfie has been hard pressed to keep up with everything since the Americans came to town. I hope you like our little village enough to stay for a while."

"Thank you. I certainly hope to, your ladyship." Bridget raised her hand in farewell, then moved farther along the bar as several clamoring voices demanded service.

Elizabeth headed for the door, anxious now to be out of the smoky, noisy atmosphere. She had some serious thinking to do, and she couldn't concentrate with all the shrill voices and raucous laughter.

The cool wind snatched at her scarf as she made her way across the car park to where she'd left her motorcycle. She tied the woolen square tighter under her chin and hitched up her skirt to climb aboard the saddle.

Somehow she just couldn't see the quiet-mannered artist taking to someone as flamboyant as the new barmaid. It just went to show there's no accounting for taste. The question uppermost in her mind, however, was why Wally Carbunkle had told her he was out of town on Sunday night, when in fact, according to the new barmaid, that very night he was singing at the piano in the Tudor Arms.

CHAPTER

❧ 10 ❧

Martin actually opened the front door when Elizabeth tugged on the ancient bell pull several minutes later. She had to help him close the door against the boisterous wind that now blew directly off the ocean and filled the hallway with the salty smell of brine.

"Nasty night out there, madam," Martin said, puffing with exertion as he slid the last bolt in place. "Looks as though we're in for another storm. I hope the wind doesn't spook the horses."

"I'm sure it won't, Martin," Elizabeth assured him. "Please tell Violet I'll be in the conservatory until the evening meal is ready."

"Yes, madam. Though I do believe that Violet is anxious to have a word with you, madam."

In the act of moving away, Elizabeth paused, "Did she say what about?"

"No, madam. She did not. But I'm praying it was to tell you she's sacked that loud-mouth hussy of a housemaid."

Elizabeth frowned. "Sadie? What has she done now?"

Martin peered at her over the gold rims of his glasses. "If you ask me, madam, the mere act of breathing is a crime where that girl is concerned."

"Oh, come now, Martin. It can't be that bad."

"She had the audacity to inform me that I wore my braces cinched too tightly, and suggested that my temperament would be greatly improved if I refrained from wearing my trousers up around my neck. At least, I gather that was the gist of her crude comments. Most of which don't bear repeating."

"Oh, dear." Elizabeth tried to prevent her lips from twitching. "I'll have a word with her, Martin."

"Thank you, madam. Not that I think it will do any good. That girl is headstrong and willful. She is disrespectful and ignores everything I say to her."

"Perhaps if you could be a little more patient with her," Elizabeth suggested, "she might be a little more amenable. I do believe she thinks highly of you, Martin."

Martin made a sound rather like an elephant clearing its throat. "Then she has a most peculiar way of showing it. The girl goes out of her way to be rude. She delights in her shocking behavior. The master would put her out in the street if he knew what was going on. Perhaps he should have a word with her, madam. The message might carry more weight coming from him."

"The master is dead, Martin. I'm the one responsible for the staff now."

Martin peered at her over his glasses. "As you say, madam."

Giving up, Elizabeth headed for the stairs. "I'll call in the kitchen to see what Violet wants then I'll be in the conservatory if anyone needs me."

"Yes, madam. Oh, and Major Monroe was asking after you as well."

"The major?" Elizabeth stopped dead in her tracks. "Did he happen to say what he wanted?"

"No, madam." Martin's voice sounded prim as he shuffled toward the library at the speed of a worm. "No doubt he will tell you that himself. He mentioned that he might call on you this evening."

Elizabeth felt like skipping as she headed for the kitchen.

Violet was in the act of taking a fruitcake from the oven when Elizabeth floated into the room a minute later. The aroma of raisins and spices made her think of Christmas.

"That smells wonderful! It's been so long since we had a fruitcake. But where did you get the eggs? I thought we'd used up all our rations for the week."

Violet stood the cake tin on the windowsill to cool. "I didn't use eggs. I used some of that dried egg powder. I don't know what it will taste like, but we'll find out soon enough."

"I'm sure it will taste wonderful, as always. I've forgotten what fruitcake tastes like. In fact, I seem to forget a lot of things lately."

"Got too much on your mind, that's the trouble." Violet dusted her hands on a tea towel and hung it back on its hook. "If you ask me, you spend far too much time doing work that would be better left to the constables. That's what they get paid for, isn't it?"

Having had this argument more times than she cared to

remember, Elizabeth refrained from commenting. "Martin told me you wanted to talk to me."

Violet joined her at the table. "It's Martin I wanted to talk to you about. I'm worried about him."

Elizabeth forgot about her ravenous appetite and stared at Violet in concern. "Is he ill?"

"Not as far as I know. At least, not in his body, though sometimes it's hard to tell. It's his mind I'm worried about. He's missing things, and this afternoon I found a lace handkerchief in his dresser drawer. I think he's giving things away to that woman. Or she's stealing them, more likely."

Elizabeth blinked. "Woman? Martin is keeping company with a woman? Who is she?"

"Her name is Beatrice Carr and he's not exactly keeping company with her." Violet paused, her head tilted on one side like a bird listening for worms. "At least, I don't think he is."

"Who is Beatrice Carr? Where did you meet her?"

"At the front door. She was selling raffle tickets."

Elizabeth shook her head in bewilderment. "What does that have to do with Martin?"

Violet rolled her eyes. "He's been *buying* them, that's what. Raffle tickets. Have you ever known Martin to spend money on anything unless he's desperate? And there's that lace handkerchief . . . and Sadie said she saw Martin talking to the suit of armor—"

Elizabeth leaned forward and tapped the table with her fingernails. "Violet, where exactly did you find the handkerchief?"

Violet raised her chin. "In his dresser. I went in his room to see if I could find his cufflinks and watch. They weren't there. What's more, his whalebone is missing, too. If you ask me, that woman is stealing him blind."

"That doesn't give you the right to go snooping around Martin's room. I think you owe him an apology."

Violet looked startled. "You're not going to tell him? I was only trying to help the old goat find his watch and cufflinks. You know how he is. I thought they'd be lying around somewhere. What I want to know is what we're going to do about this Beatrice Carr."

"Nothing." Elizabeth rose to her feet. "What Martin does in his spare time is his business. I think we should allow him that privilege."

Violet frowned. "This is Martin we're talking about, Lizzie. He's not capable of taking care of his business himself. We have to look out for him. I asked him about the woman. He says he doesn't remember buying any raffle tickets."

"All right." Elizabeth paused at the door. "I'll talk to him, though I think you're worrying about nothing. Martin has probably found a new place to keep his things and has forgotten where he put them."

"Well, there's something else to think about. Sadie says there's a rumor going around that there's a German spy in the village. Wouldn't surprise me if Beatrice Carr is a spy."

Elizabeth fought the urge to laugh out loud. "That ridiculous rumor started with Rita Crumm. I really don't think we need worry about it, do you? Even if it were true, I really don't think a German spy could possibly be interested in anything that Martin might have in his room."

"You never know," Violet muttered, obviously put out at not being taken seriously. "Stranger things have happened."

"Well, I'll talk to Martin, though I'm quite sure we

have nothing to worry about. In the meantime, I'll be in the conservatory if anyone needs me."

Violet cocked her head to one side again. "You mean if the major comes looking for you, don't you?"

Elizabeth let the door close behind her without answering. She wasn't in the mood for Violet's meaningful comments, even if they were well meant. This talk of spies and missing items was unsettling, and right now all she wanted was to spend a few quiet moments in the sanctuary of her favorite room with a glass of sherry. And if Earl Monroe put in an appearance, well, that would make her entire day that much brighter.

When the light tap on the door came a half hour later, Elizabeth jumped so violently she knew she'd been waiting for that sound ever since she'd settled down in the conservatory.

Earl's head appeared around the door, and his smile seemed to warm the room. "Am I disturbing you? I was going to check with Violet or Martin, but I figured you'd be in here." He walked all the way in and closed the door behind him. "Or is that not the proper protocol?"

"To blazes with protocol." Surprised at herself, Elizabeth held out her hand. "It's always good to see you, Earl."

She was enchanted when he raised her fingers to his lips. "At least I can do this right."

She laughed to cover her confusion. "Very gallant of you, Major. I trust you've had a good day?"

His smile faded as he sat down next to her on the wicker couch. "We lost two planes today."

Immediately she reached out to briefly touch his hand, then thought better of it. "Oh, Earl, I'm so terribly sorry.

Were they . . . did they . . . ?" Unable to finish the sentence, she could only gaze helplessly into his face.

"One went down in flames. They never got out. The crew bailed out of the other one, so we're hoping . . ." His shrug finished the sentence for him.

Wishing there were something she could say, anything that would take away the sudden bleakness in his eyes, she picked up the bottle of scotch she always kept waiting for him, just in case he should come to see her. "Can I pour you a glass?"

"Sure, thanks." He leaned back, his hands behind his head. "So what have you been up to lately? Not still chasing after murderers, I hope?"

"Not exactly." She poured out the scotch and handed it to him. "Though I did find out that at least two recent visitors to the village were in the vicinity at the time of the murder." The memory of her conversation with the barmaid prompted her to add, "Maybe three. Though I suppose he doesn't count, since he lives right next door."

Earl swallowed a mouthful of scotch. "Doesn't that sea captain, what's his name, Carbunkle, live in the cottage next door?"

"Yes, he does. He told me he was out of town on the night before Mr. Thorncroft was killed, and therefore wasn't there early the next morning to witness anything that might help find the killer. But then Bridget, the new barmaid at the Tudor Arms, told me he was in the bar on Sunday night, apparently entertaining everyone with his singing."

"Maybe he just forgot."

"It's only been two days. I have the distinct feeling that there's something Captain Carbunkle doesn't want to tell me."

"About the murder?"

"I hope not. I can't imagine Wally Carbunkle involved in murder, yet I can't think why he would deliberately lie about his whereabouts that night."

"Why don't you ask him?"

Elizabeth sighed. "I suppose I should. If Wally is in some kind of trouble, I must do what I can to help."

"Or better yet," Earl said, with a hint of reprimand in his voice, "let the constables talk to him. It is their job, after all."

"I'm not sure it is." She gazed unhappily at her favorite copy of a Monet that hung on the wall. "I don't think even George knows much about the investigation. There's so much mystery surrounding this case. I really would like to know exactly what is going on."

Earl put down his glass. "Then you *are* conducting your own investigation."

"Just asking a few questions, that's all." She smiled at him. "Violet brought back one of Mr. Thorncroft's paintings this morning. A rather nice seascape. Though I wish he hadn't taken liberties with the scenery. The Tudor Arms looks most odd perched on the edge of the cliffs."

Earl gave her a stern look. "Don't change the subject. You know how I feel about you getting involved in murder. It's dangerous."

She gazed steadily at him. "I'm very good at taking care of myself."

"Granted. You're also impulsive, and a mite reckless at times. It's gotten you into trouble more than once."

"And each time you've most valiantly come to my rescue. I should bestow upon you a white horse and maybe that suit of armor in the great hall. I think you would look very dashing in that."

"Elizabeth, this is no laughing matter. I care about what happens to you."

She sobered at once. "I know," she said softly. "That means a great deal to me."

He looked down at his hands, and once more her heart started thumping in a ridiculous manner. It seemed an eternity before he spoke. "Elizabeth, I don't have any right to dictate what you do. It's none of my business. But someone has to watch out for you. Someone a little more capable than Violet or Martin. I guess I feel responsible for you. That might not be what you want, but it's how I feel. So give me a break, okay? Let me worry about you."

Her throat ached with the effort to answer him in a light tone. "I'm happy to know someone worries about me, Earl, but you really have nothing to worry about. I'm simply talking to a few people, that's all. Something I do all the time."

He continued to study her long enough to make her uncomfortable, then finally nodded. "Okay. Just promise me, that if you get so much as a whiff of a clue about the murder, you'll tell me."

"The very first whiff." She smiled serenely at him. "I promise."

He seemed unconvinced, but nevertheless reached for his glass again. "Great. Now tell me about this painting. What was this about the pub being on the cliffs?"

She told him, and thus followed a long and invigorating discussion on classic art and its influence on modern artists. The hour sped by, and she was disappointed when Violet appeared to announce supper was ready.

Earl, much to her dismay, declined her invitation to join them, saying he had business to take care of at the base. As always when he left her, she committed the image of his beloved face to memory, just in case it should be the last time she saw him. As always, he left an empty space on her heart when he disappeared from view.

Later that evening, she carried Basil Thorncroft's painting to her bedroom in order to examine it again. Earl had been quite adamant in his assertion that most modern artists subconsciously copied the style of the masters, instead of experimenting with their own unique expressions of their talent.

Wondering which artist Basil Thorncroft might have emulated, she studied the detail on the canvas. The brush strokes were reminiscent of Van Gogh, though not as choppy. The whitecaps on the ocean were fairly symmetrical, something Van Gogh would never have depicted.

Her gaze wandered across the canvas, then paused, caught by an odd shadow in the depths of the ocean. She moved the picture closer to her bedside lamp for a better look. There it was—a long gray shape painted quite deliberately, and not just a careless sweep of the brush as she'd first thought.

What was it? She held the canvas up higher and tilted it this way and that to catch the light. Was it a whale? But as far as she knew, there were no whales in the North Sea. Besides, it didn't look like a whale. It looked more like a . . . she peered closer, excitement stabbing her . . . yes. It looked like a submarine.

Her hands trembled as she lowered the painting to the bed. Could it possibly be a submarine? But if Basil Thorncroft had seen one, wouldn't he be the first to raise an alarm?

She began pacing back and forth across the carpet, wrestling with the thoughts tumbling through her mind. What if the rumors were true and there really was a spy in Sitting Marsh? Could he have arrived by submarine? Had Basil Thorncroft seen him? Was that why he was killed? It would explain why the investigation had been taken over by someone *higher up*. The War Office, perhaps. Or the Secret Service.

Elizabeth stopped pacing, her excitement so intense she could hardly breathe. She was remembering Sid saying that the investigation was secret, and George butting in. Sid could have actually been going to say Secret Service, and George bounced in to cut him off.

Then there was that odd comment from Sid when she'd mentioned Basil Thorncroft as being an innocent man caught in a crime. He'd obviously lied about the artist being a heavy drinker. Those two had something up their sleeves all right.

Convinced she was on to something, Elizabeth climbed into bed, promising herself that the very next morning she would go down to talk to George again. And this time she wouldn't let him evade her questions.

She fell asleep, warm in the knowledge that Earl Monroe cared enough about her to be concerned for her safety, and if nothing else, would be there to protect her in her hour of need. It wasn't much, compared to all she longed to have, but for now, it was enough.

CHAPTER

❀ 11 ❀

The next morning Elizabeth stopped by her office before going into town. She wanted to make sure Polly sent out the rent notices, which were due at the end of the month. Much to her surprise, Polly had already written out the notices and addressed the envelopes. All that remained was for Elizabeth to attach her signature to the bottom of each page.

She did so, impressed by her assistant's competence. She'd had serious doubts when Polly had first approached her with the idea of helping her out in the office, but she had to admit the child had become quite an asset.

"You are doing a wonderful job, Polly," she told the smiling young woman. "I really can't imagine what I'd do without you now."

"Thank you, m'm." Polly dipped a little curtsey, reminding Elizabeth of Bridget the day before. "I'm glad
you're pleased with me. I do try and I do like working
here in the office."

"Then we're both happy."

"Oh, while I remember, m'm, someone called this
morning about the cottage in Sandhill Lane. He's coming
by later to fill out an application."

Elizabeth put the cap back on her fountain pen and
replaced it in its holder. "Oh, really. Did he leave his
name?"

"Yes, m'm. It was . . ." Polly moved over to the desk
and picked up a small scrap of paper. "Here it is. Mr.
Douglas McNally."

*McNally. The man whom Bridget told her was asking
about land.* "Very well," she said out loud. "Did he say
what time he would be here? I'll need to interview him."

"This afternoon, m'm. After lunch, he said."

Elizabeth rose to her feet, and made a mental note to
be back well before then. She paused on her way to the
door. "Oh, by the way, I met the new barmaid yesterday.
She seems very nice."

"Bridget? Yes, m'm. I like her."

"She mentioned that Marlene was seeing Peter Weston.
How is that going?"

Polly shrugged. "All right, I s'pose. Marlene won't talk
about him much. I don't think she knows enough about
him to talk about him. All I hope is that he isn't the spy
what's hiding in the village."

Elizabeth paused. "Spy? Oh, yes, Violet mentioned
something about a rumor last night."

"It's more than a rumor, m'm," Polly said earnestly.
"Sid's wife told Marlene that the bigwigs in London think
a spy killed Mr. Thorncroft. That's why they're looking

into the case. 'Course, Ethel Goffin wasn't supposed to tell no one, but she said that if there was a spy running around Sitting Marsh, everyone should know about it, so's they could catch him."

"I see." Chagrined that she hadn't paid more attention to the rumor earlier, Elizabeth strode to the door. "Though I can't imagine what a spy would find so interesting about Sitting Marsh."

"It isn't Sitting Marsh the spy's interested in. They reckon it's the American base he's after."

Elizabeth felt a sharp chill. Of course. If plans for future missions fell into the wrong hands, it could spell disaster for the American bombers. Now she had an even more important reason for knowing how the investigation was going. It had just become a personal issue.

George was not at his usual position behind the desk when Elizabeth entered the police station later. She sat herself down on the visitor's chair—an outdated and somewhat decrepit piece of furniture that had definitely seen better days. She was resigned for a long wait. Heaven only knew how long it would take the doddery constables to conduct whatever business had taken them both out of their station, leaving it unattended.

No more than a few dull minutes passed, however, before the door opened and both men wandered in, each clutching a large bag from Bessie's Bake Shop.

Sid seemed startled to see her, and dropped his elevenses on the counter as if it were a crime to be holding them. George, on the other hand, wore an expression that warned Elizabeth he was on guard and would probably refuse to answer her questions.

She folded her hands demurely in her lap and smiled

at both of them. "Good morning, gentlemen. I trust you are both well?"

Sid stuttered something, but George seemed quite unperturbed by her presence.

"We was just about to have a spot of tea and crumpets, your ladyship. Would you care to join us?"

"Oh, thank you, George. Actually, I was on my way to see Captain Carbunkle. I just dropped in to see if there were any new developments in the murder investigation."

Sid picked up his bag of crumpets and murmuring, "If you'll excuse me, your ladyship," scurried into the back office, leaving the door open behind him.

George cleared his throat. "I already explained to you, Lady Elizabeth. As far as Sid and me are concerned, there isn't no investigation."

Elizabeth frowned. "Are you telling me now that no one is trying to find out who killed poor Mr. Thorncroft?"

"I didn't exactly say that, m'm."

"Then what are you saying, George?"

"I'm not saying nothing, your ladyship. As I told you yesterday, my lips are sealed, so to speak."

"Yes, you said it was a secret." She watched George's face closely as she spoke, and was satisfied to see a flicker of apprehension in his eyes. "You weren't talking about the Secret Service, by any chance?"

A deep flush spread across George's face, darkening already ruddy cheeks. "S-Secret Service, your ladyship? Whatever gave you that idea?" His laugh was high-pitched and blatantly forced.

Elizabeth leaned forward. "George, was Basil Thorncroft a spy?"

George's voice rose even higher. "Spy? Of course not. That's the most stupid . . . beg your pardon, m'm, but Basil Thorncroft was no spy. I can swear to that."

She heard just enough conviction in his voice to reassure her. "Well then, if he wasn't a spy, was he, perhaps, killed by one?"

George's sparse white eyebrows jerked up and down. "I don't know what you're talking about, Lady Elizabeth. All this talk about spies is beyond me. I never heard anything about there being a spy."

A choking sound came from the back room, where Sid was apparently enjoying his toasted crumpet.

"And neither has Sid," George added, loud enough for his voice to carry to the back room.

The choking stopped immediately.

"Are you saying you haven't heard the rumors about a spy hiding in Sitting Marsh?"

George's face was still flushed, but he met her gaze steadily enough. "Someone, whose name I won't mention, was talking out of turn, that's all. I'd venture to say, m'm, that rumors are better ignored. Most of them are nothing more than flights of fancy."

"Most of them," Elizabeth murmured. "But not all."

"Depends on what you want to believe, I suppose, your ladyship."

Elizabeth rose, pausing in front of his desk to lean a hand on it. "I suppose it's up to me to find out what to believe. I'll tell you this, George. If there is a spy in the village, I would think it our duty to find out who he is, before someone else ends up as tragically as poor Mr. Thorncroft."

"There are people taking care of that, m'm."

"Then you are admitting there *is* a spy in Sitting Marsh?"

"I'm admitting no such thing, your ladyship. I'm only saying that this murder case is in the hands of some pretty important people, and if we know what's good for us, we'll keep our noses out of it. And that's all I'm going to say on the subject."

Elizabeth knew when she'd hit a brick wall. She wasn't going to get much more out of George, even if he knew more, which she doubted. There seemed little doubt now that the rumors about a spy carried some weight, but George wasn't about to confirm it.

The question now was if the spy had been responsible for Basil Thorncroft's death, and if so, why. Even more crucial, had he left the village, or was he still lurking around, waiting for an opportunity to break into the American base?

That was something that needed to be ascertained as soon as possible. It was imperative. And she wasn't going to wait around for some invisible secret agent to find out what she wanted to know. The first thing she had to do was warn Earl about a possible break-in, and then she needed to talk to both Peter Weston and Doug McNally. They, and the close-lipped bird-watcher, were strangers in town, and were the logical place to start. But first, she needed to talk to Captain Carbunkle. While the idea of him being an enemy spy was quite ludicrous, there was still the matter of him lying about his whereabouts the night the murder occurred, and she wanted very much to know what it was he wasn't telling her.

She set off up the hill to Sandhill Lane, trying to ignore the little voice in her head that echoed George's warning. *If we know what's good for us, we'll keep our noses out of it.* It was her duty after all, and her tenants depended on her. If her desire to protect the citizens of Sitting Marsh got her into trouble, so be it. She would worry about that if and when it happened.

•　•　•

Rita Crumm's tiny front room sounded like a school playground at midmorning playtime. Rita was beginning to think that she'd made a grave mistake in holding the Housewives League meeting in her house. For one thing, the room was too small to fit the dozen or so women, most of whom were overweight to start with. There weren't enough chairs, and worse, she didn't have enough matching cups and saucers to serve them all tea. That was bound to raise a few noses.

For another thing, the three women lining up to use the lavatory were blocking her narrow hallway, making it impossible for Marge Gunther and Nellie Smith to get from the front door into the front room. Everyone seemed to be talking at once, all of them competing to be heard, until Rita was quite sure she was about to lose her mind, never mind her temper.

Having finally had enough of Marge's strident demands that somebody shift their bum out of the way to let her through, Rita abandoned her attempts to behave with decorum and let loose with one of her famous bellows. "Everyone shut their mouth . . . *now!*"

The chattering miraculously died to a furtive whisper or two, and an unforgivable giggle that earned the unfortunate woman a glare designed to cut her in half. "Now," Rita announced when she finally had everyone's undivided attention, "find a seat. All of you. The younger ones can sit on the floor. Joan! Get yourself out of that lavatory. You've been in there long enough to drown yourself."

The door to the bathroom flew open and a red-faced Joan emerged, muttering under her breath.

A uneasy semblance of order finally being restored, Rita climbed over several pairs of pudgy knees to get to the center of the room. Aware that even she couldn't hold the ladies' attention for long, she came straight, and quite dramatically, she thought, to the point.

"As everyone knows by now, there's a spy lurking around in Sitting Marsh. Since no one seems to be doing anything about it, I propose that we, the Housewives League of Sitting Marsh, track him down and bring him to justice."

A chorus of shocked exclamations answered her startling announcement.

"What! Are you daft?"

"You want to get us all killed?"

"What spy? What's she talking about? I didn't know there was a spy."

This last comment from Florrie Evans, a wide-eyed, jittery woman with chewed nails, brought a hail of derision from her companions.

"Wake up, Flo!"

"Where you been the last two days? Hiding under your blinking bed?"

"Quiet!" Rita's roar silenced even Marge. "We not only know there *is* a spy, we know who the spy is, don't we."

"Do we?"

"Who? Who's she talking about?"

"Buggered if I know."

Rita gritted her teeth. "Do I really have to remind you who we saw on the cliffs the other morning, looking out to sea with binoculars?"

"The bird-watcher!" Marge clapped her hands. "I knew he was the spy. I told Lady Elizabeth he was the spy."

Attention immediately shifted in her direction. "Go on! What'd she say?"

Marge shrugged. "She got all hoity-toity like she does sometimes. Said if he was really a spy, he wouldn't be that obvious. Told me not to worry about it."

"Which is exactly what P.C. Dalrymple said when I told him what we'd seen." Rita huffed out her breath in disgust. "He wouldn't listen to anything I said and had the nerve to tell me I was imagining things. Me, the only person in this village who has the intelligence and fortitude to fight this war single-handedly on the home front. There wouldn't be a Housewives League if it wasn't for me. There'd be no bottle cap collection, no knitted woollies for the forces, no—"

Marge yawned loudly, and Rita glared at her before continuing, "If we're going after the bird-watcher, we have to make plans and do it now. We can't waste any time."

"What'll we do?" someone asked. "Shoot him?"

"No, we're not going to shoot him." Rita paused for effect. Much to her satisfaction, everyone was silent now, waiting for her next words. "What we're going to do," she said, drawing each word out to savor the suspense as long as she could, "is surprise him. We're going to go up to him, grab him, and tie him up."

"And then we'll all have our way with him," Nellie announced with relish.

A chorus of groans and cat calls filled the room.

Rita silenced them with a lifted hand. "What we have to do is make him confess that he's a spy, or those twits down at the police station won't arrest him."

"How are we going to do that?" Marge demanded. "He's not going to tell us nothing and why should he? I know I wouldn't if I was a spy."

"Me neither!"

"No one would, would they. Be blooming daft, that's what I say."

Rita easily overpowered the doubting voices. "Then we have to *make* him tell us. Even if we have to torture him, like they do in the German prison camps." The utter silence that followed this comment was unsettling and she cleared her throat. "It's the only way we can prove he's the spy."

"Torture him?" Florrie clutched her neck, making her voice even more quavery than usual. "How are we going to do that?"

"Poke at him with sticks?" someone suggested.

Florrie moaned. "I think I'm going to be sick."

Rita had to admit, her stomach felt a bit queasy at the thought. The more she thought about the actual performance of the operation, the less palatable the whole idea seemed.

"We could march him down to the police station and let *them* torture him," someone suggested.

Marge sighed. "Why don't we just turn the tables on him?"

Rita eyed her with suspicion. "Like what?"

"Well, we all spy on him and watch what he does, and then when we see him spying on someone else, we can tell George and Sid and let them take care of him."

Several women nodded and murmured agreement with obvious relief.

Although reluctant to give up her ambitious plan and subsequent promise of glory over the capture of an enemy spy, Rita had to admit the idea was a lot more comfortable on her stomach. She was prepared to go a long way for the sake of the war effort and the salvation of her country, but when it came right down to it, torture was a little bit too Nazi-ish.

She wasn't, however, prepared to let Marge take credit for the idea. "Exactly what I was going to suggest. Yes, we'll spy on him and catch him in the act. Florrie, do you

still have that box camera you were lugging around all
last summer?"

Florrie nodded, eager to please now that the immediate
threat of losing her breakfast seemed to be passing. "I
think I've still got some film left for it."

"Good. Go and fetch it and meet us at the top of the
coast road. We'll spread out along the cliffs and wait for
the spy to turn up. We'll creep along behind the hedges
so he won't see us coming."

"How will we see him if we're behind the hedges?"
Florrie asked nervously.

"You look through the holes, silly," Nellie said.

"What if there aren't any holes?"

"You poke a hole in the hedge yourself, don't you."
Rita was beginning to lose her patience again. "For
Gawd's sake, Florrie, use your bloomin' loaf. There's a
war on, remember? We've all got to stick together in this
or we'll fail." She struck a pose and punched the air with
her fist. "Remember the oath of the Housewives League.
One for all and all for one!"

The members of that elite organization answered her
with ragged echoes and with far less enthusiasm than Rita
would have liked. Nevertheless, she was satisfied with her
progress. She and her trusty warriors were hot on the trail
of the enemy, and her excitement knew no bounds.

By the end of the day she could be famous, with her
name in all the papers. This could be the day the War
Office sat up and took notice of her efforts. Those know-
it-alls up there in London weren't the only ones who
could do a great service for their country and earn the
undying gratitude and respect of Mr. Churchill himself.

She could see herself now, standing in the Houses of
Parliament while Winnie pinned the medal on her coat.

He'd stand back and salute, and she'd salute him right back. Then he'd shake her hand and say . . .

"Here, get out of the way, Rita. I've got to go and piddle."

Rita blinked, her daydream vanishing as Marge shoved by her to get to the door. The other women were struggling to their feet, not one of them looking as if they were ready to tackle an enemy spy. For a moment Rita's confidence wavered, then she pulled her shoulders back. She wasn't in charge of the Housewives League for nothing. She'd show them all what she could do. She was going to capture a German spy if she had to do it all by herself.

CHAPTER

❀ 12 ❀

As luck would have it, Wally Carbunkle was emerging from his garden gate when Elizabeth sailed into the lane on her motorcycle. She raised a hand to him, then shut off the engine and swung her leg expertly over the saddle without showing too much leg beneath her pleated skirt.

"Just the person I wanted to see," she called out when it seemed that Wally would scuttle off down the lane without talking to her.

"Is there something I can do for you, your ladyship?" he asked as he reluctantly approached and pulled his cap from his head. "I was just off for me pint at the Arms. I like to get there before the midday rush, otherwise it's hard to get a seat at the window. I don't like sitting anywhere without a window. Used to looking over the rail of a ship all me life, that's the trouble. Makes me feel too shut in, if you know what I mean. I—"

"I do know what you mean, Captain," Elizabeth said firmly, in an effort to stop the flow of conversation. She had the idea Wally was talking too fast because he was afraid of what she was about to ask him. "As a matter of fact, it was about the Tudor Arms that I wanted to talk to you."

Wally's face seemed to close up. "Is that so? Well, I don't know what help I can be. Not too familiar with what goes on down there, actually. I just go in and have me pint and keep meself to meself."

"Really?" Elizabeth drew her brows together. "I was under the impression that you did a great deal more at the pub. For instance, I heard that you led the customers in a rousing chorus of sea shanties last Sunday night. Bridget told me all about it. She was most complimentary."

"Talks entirely too much, that woman," Wally muttered. "Women shouldn't be working behind a bar. Never did know how to keep their traps shut."

Ignoring this slur on the female population, Elizabeth murmured, "Didn't you tell me you were out of town on Sunday night?"

Wally's cheeks took on a purple hue. "Did I? Can't remember, your ladyship. Memory's a bit hazy these days. Comes of spending so many days out on the seas. You have no idea how that can affect your mind. Why, I remember once—"

"Wally," Elizabeth said quietly. "We've been friends for a long time. If you're in some kind of trouble, I hope that you would feel free to confide in an old friend. You know that I would do my best to help you."

"Trouble?" The captain's eyes rolled frantically around

in his head. "Don't know what you're talking about, your ladyship. I'm not in any trouble. Not me."

"It's not like you to lie to me."

Wally jammed his cap back on his head at a rather jaunty angle. "Begging your pardon, your ladyship, but I didn't realize that I was obliged to report my actions to you. Where I was and what I was doing on Sunday night is my own business and nobody's else's."

"Under normal circumstances, yes," Elizabeth agreed. "But a brutal murder has been committed in the cottage right next door to you. I'm sure you are as anxious as I am to see the culprit apprehended. I'm surprised the investigators haven't questioned you already."

"If you must know, Lady Elizabeth, the investigator did question me as to my whereabouts. He seemed quite satisfied with my answers."

This was not going well at all, Elizabeth realized. Obviously she would learn nothing more from the captain, and she had no wish to antagonize him further. "All I really meant to ask was if you've had an opportunity to talk to some of the people staying at the Tudor Arms," she said, hoping her smile would be enough to placate the indignant man. "I have met Mr. Whitton myself, but as yet I haven't made the acquaintance of Mr. Weston or Mr. McNally. Though I will be interviewing Mr. McNally this afternoon. He might very well turn out to be your new neighbor, if all goes well."

Wally Carbunkle looked only slightly appeased, but he answered her calmly enough. "I haven't met any of the gentlemen you've mentioned. I hope your interview goes well."

"Thank you. So do I." Elizabeth grasped the handlebars of her motorcycle and eased her leg across the saddle.

"Please forgive me, Wally, if I spoke out of turn. You know I only have your best interests at heart."

Wally nodded. "Quite so, your ladyship."

Elizabeth revved the engine and, with a final wave at the captain, moved off down the lane. It was fairly obvious that Wally Carbunkle was hiding something that he didn't want her to know. She could only hope he wasn't implicated in the murder of poor Mr. Thorncroft, and whatever reason he had to lie about his whereabouts on Sunday night was something far more innocent.

Douglas McNally, a sturdy man with reddish hair and piercing blue eyes, waited for her to sit behind her desk before seating himself in her office that afternoon. He was actually quite different from the image Elizabeth had conjured up. For one thing, he was much younger than she'd imagined. No more than thirty, if that. Just a year or two younger than herself. For another, he seemed a very straightforward young man, looking her directly in the eye and seemingly unperturbed by her title, which she rather admired.

"Our greengrocer's name is McNally," she told him after politely refusing his offer of a cigarette. "Harold McNally. I don't suppose you're related in any way?"

The young man opposite her shook his head. "Not as far as I know. It's a common enough name in Scotland. You shout it out on a busy street and fifty people will either rush toward you or run for their lives."

His thick Scottish brogue and wry sense of humor delighted her, and he was very frank about his reason for being in Sitting Marsh. "I'm looking for land to build a munitions factory," he explained. "My company in Glasgow has been contracted to build several of them, and I'm scouting around for suitable locations. I plan on spending at least three months here in Sitting Marsh, maybe longer. I know that's only short term for rental purposes, but if we decide to build here, I'll be around for much longer than that."

Elizabeth decided to be just as frank. "Mr. McNally, while I understand that such factories are essential, I have to warn you that the residents of Sitting Marsh will not take this lightly. I doubt very much if anyone would be willing to sell you land for that purpose. There are too many factors against it."

"I'm not planning on buying land, your ladyship. My company would lease it. Whoever owned the land would be paid a considerable sum of money for as long as the factory was in use. When the war is over, if the factory is no longer needed, it may either be torn down or converted to something else. Either way, the landowner would keep his land."

"I see." The offer was extremely tempting. For more than two years she'd struggled to keep up with the ceaseless repairs to the mansion as well as the costs of running such a vast home. It had been extremely difficult to keep up appearances in spite of everything. She was determined to keep the sorry state of her financial affairs a secret from her tenants. There was so much insecurity in wartime, the last thing they needed was to worry about their homes.

Nevertheless, the prospect of a munitions factory on the Wellsborough estate was unthinkable. Her father would certainly come back to haunt her if she were to agree to such a travesty. "I'm sorry, Mr. McNally," she said with genuine regret, "I must tell you I think you are wasting your time. Most of the vacant land in this area is owned by the Wellsborough estate, and I would never give permission for a factory to be built. Much of the rest is owned by farmers, and the council members are likely to protest strongly to anyone offering land for such a project."

McNally shook his head in disbelief. "This is a small village. Think of what the factory could do for the people living here. It would bring more people to the area, which would mean more houses, shops, a new school perhaps, more work for everyone."

Elizabeth sighed. "We have enough trouble keeping up with everything now, with the vast majority of our men serving in the forces. Most of these people don't want change. They like their lives the way they are."

"The older people, right?" McNally leaned forward, his eyes gleaming with a restless energy that Elizabeth found oddly disturbing. "What about the younger ones, Lady Elizabeth? Leaving the village as soon as they're old enough, I don't doubt. Aye, I've seen it happen often enough. Nothing to keep them here, so they're off to the cities to find a new life. Maybe if you have something better to offer them here in Sitting Marsh, they wouldn't be so anxious to leave."

"It's not only that. One has to regard the possibility of making the village a target area for the enemy. At present, the Germans have no need to attack us."

"You have an American base within two miles of here."

Elizabeth pursed her lips and folded her hands on the desk in front of her. "I can't speak for everyone, of course. I can only speak for myself. I've already told you where I stand on this issue. The subject would have to be taken up with the council should you find someone willing to accept your offer. If you still want to pursue the project, you are welcome to rent the cottage. Though I must ask for a three-month lease, at least."

Douglas McNally beamed, and rose to his feet. "Done.

And I thank you, your ladyship. I promise to stay out of your hair as much as possible."

It wasn't her hair she was worrying about, Elizabeth thought as she, too, rose from her chair. It was the hairs on the heads of every one of her villagers. Something told her that she could be asking for trouble by encouraging this young man in his endeavors, yet in spite of her reservations, she liked him. Perhaps, even if he couldn't find the land for his factory, he might grow to like Sitting Marsh well enough to stay. That was if the villagers didn't run him out of town as soon as they found out his purpose.

"You're seeing far too much of that young man," Edna Barnett declared. "You've seen him two nights in a row and now you're going out with him again tonight. It's too much, especially when you don't know nothing about him."

She was on her knees in the living room blacking the fireplace grate and had to look up at her elder daughter. It put her at a distinct disadvantage. It was a little hard to lay down the law with a crick in her neck.

Marlene tossed her hair back with a flick of her head. Edna always admired how she did that. Nice hair, Marlene had. Most girls would kill to have that shade of red and that natural curl. Marlene didn't know how lucky she was.

"Don't go on, Ma. I know enough about Pete Weston to know he's a nice bloke. At least he doesn't paw at me like them bloomin' Yanks."

Edna sat back on her heels and stared at her daughter. "You let those Americans paw at you? How could you, Marlene! You was brought up better than that."

Marlene grinned. "I didn't *let* them, Ma. That's the point. I had to spend all my time fighting them off. I don't have to do that with Pete." She got a dreamy look on her face that frightened Edna. "He's a perfect gentleman. Perfect in every way."

"Has he told you any more about himself? Where he lives, who his parents are, why he's in Sitting Marsh, why he isn't in the army?"

Marlene got that stubborn look that Edna dreaded. "He's told me all he needs to tell me, Ma. I've only known him two days. There's plenty of time for him to tell me more about himself. Right now I'm just happy he wants to go out with me. With his money and looks, he could have any girl he wants."

"Well, I think there's something fishy about him. I mean, what's a man like that doing hanging around here? There's nothing for him in Sitting Marsh, unless he's up to no good. You know what Ethel Goffin said about there being a spy in the village."

Marlene's laugh sounded forced. "You're not telling me you think Pete is a German spy? I've never heard anything so daft in me whole life."

Edna put her frustration into her polishing cloth as she attacked the grate. It was hard bringing up two girls with their father away in the war. What with the Americans flashing their money around and turning their heads, and now strangers coming into town and nobody knowing what they were doing there. It was all very worrying.

"You worry too much, Ma," Marlene said, echoing her mother's thoughts. "I'm a big girl, I can take care of myself. If you want someone to worry about, then pick on Polly for a change. She's still mooning over her Sam, and he's breaking her blinking heart. I keep telling her she's wasting her life over him but she won't listen to me."

"Polly'll come to her senses soon enough." Edna grunted as she climbed to her feet. Her arthritis was getting worse every day. "She's young. She'll get tired of waiting around for him and she'll go looking for someone else. I never did approve of him anyway. He's much too old for our Polly."

"You're always finding excuses to hate our boyfriends." Marlene finished sewing the button on her blouse and bit off the thread with her teeth. "No one's ever good enough for us if we listen to you."

"I just want you both to be happy." Edna's lower lip trembled and she caught it between her teeth for a moment. "You two are all I've got until your father comes home."

The resentment in Marlene's face vanished. She slung the blouse over her arm, and wound her free arm around her mother's shoulders. "I know you miss Dad, Ma. But he'll be home again one day soon, you'll see. Don't you worry about Polly and me. We'll be all right. Promise." Her lips touched Edna's cheek, then she was clattering up the stairs to her bedroom.

Edna winced as the door upstairs slammed shut. She did her best, she told herself as she headed for the kitchen. That was all she could do. Maybe she should join the Women's Volunteers. Might take her mind off her troubles. As for Marlene, she had to grow up sometime. She just hoped this Pete Weston didn't break her daughter's heart, like that boy broke Polly's. One miserable face moping round the house was quite enough.

Sadie paused, holding her dart in midair. She'd just seen Marlene come into the pub with her new boyfriend. After all Polly had said about him, Sadie was really anxious to meet the bloke.

"Come on, honey, let her fly. We're due back at the base in a couple of hours."

Sadie grinned at the wiry GI impatiently waiting for his

turn. "What's your hurry, Yank? You ain't going to win anyway, so you might as well give up now."

"Oh, yeah? Who says?"

For answer, Sadie flicked her wrist and the dart thudded into the narrow outer circle. "There you are, what'd I tell you! That's me double, me old mate. The game's mine."

The American groaned amid jeers from his companions. "Okay, okay. I wanna return match."

"Later." Sadie pulled her darts from the dartboard and slipped them into their case. "I got business to attend to right now."

The jeers turned to whistles and laughter. Ignoring the crude comments, Sadie pushed through the crowd of Americans and headed for the bar. Marlene and Pete were seated at a corner table, heads together, whispering to each other across a flickering candle. Sadie felt a pang of envy as she tried to catch Bridget's eye. It must be nice to have a bloke that much interested in what you had to say.

Bridget finally stomped over to her. "Okay, what'll you have?"

Sadie jerked a thumb over her shoulder at Marlene's table. "What are they drinking?"

"A pint of bitter and a gin and orange."

"I'll have two gin and oranges and a pint of bitter, please."

Bridget looked surprised. "You're buying the drinks? Did you win on the horses, or something?"

Sadie made a face. "Nah, never been lucky with gambling. I can win more money playing darts. That's if the buggers ever pay up. That lot over there owe me a couple of quid already."

Bridget's eyebrows lifted. "Two pounds? That's a lot of money."

"Not to the Yanks, it ain't." Sadie grinned. "Gawd help me if I ever lose, though."

Bridget dumped a foaming glass tankard on the counter. "One beer. Two gins coming up."

Sadie watched her pour the gin into each glass and top it with orange juice. "Have you met him yet?"

"Who, Pete? Yeah, he was down here lunchtime. I was busy, though, so I didn't have time to talk to him too much. Posh bloke, isn't he. Talks as if he's got a mouthful of marbles. I haven't met her yet. Who is she?"

"Polly's sister, Marlene. She works in the hairdresser's in the High Street." Sadie eyed the bright ginger mess that crowned Bridget's head, making her look like a worn-out scouring pad. "She's really good if you want someone to do your hair."

Bridget patted the fuzz as if she thought she was Betty Grable posing for a picture. "Oh, I do my own hair."

"Yeah. I noticed." Sadie glanced back at the couple at the table. "What's he like, this Pete Weston? Polly thinks he's strange. She doesn't like him at all."

Bridget shrugged. "He's all right. Doesn't say much about himself. I think he might be wanting to move here. He's always asking questions about the village. Though I can't think why someone with his background would want to bury himself down here in this miserable hole."

"I thought you liked living in Sitting Marsh."

"Not really. It's too quiet. I like a place with a bit more excitement. I don't plan on being around that much longer, anyway."

"Go on! That's too bad. We'll miss you."

Bridget looked worried. "Do me a favor. Don't tell anyone. I don't want to say anything to Alfie until I know when I'm leaving. I don't want him replacing me before I'm ready."

Sadie put a finger over her lips. "Mum's the word. So where you going? London?"

Bridget barked a short laugh. "Not on your bloody life. Too many bombs going off for my liking."

"Not half there isn't. What with Hitler dropping all them unexploded bombs everywhere, you never know when one'll go off. So where you going then?"

"I haven't made up my mind yet." Bridget nodded at the couple in the corner. "Those two look like they're sharing some big dark secret."

Sadie glanced at the customers on either side of her, both of whom seemed engrossed in their companions' conversations. She beckoned to Bridget to come closer, then hissed in the barmaid's ear. "Polly thinks he might be that spy what's hanging around the village."

The glasses at Bridget's elbow clinked together, spilling some of their contents. "What spy?" she said, her voice rising a notch or two.

Sadie stared at her in disbelief. "You haven't heard about the spy? I thought everyone knew about it. He's the one what's supposed to have killed that artist in Lady Elizabeth's cottage."

Bridget shook her head and grabbed a cloth. "No, I didn't know." She swiped at the small puddle of booze on the counter. "I spilled some. Let me get you some more."

Sadie waited while Bridget topped off the glasses and replaced the bottle on the shelf. "I wouldn't worry too much about it," she said when the barmaid turned back to her. "Lady Elizabeth is looking into it, and I heard she's really clever at solving murders. If there's a spy in the village and he killed Mr. Thorncroft, I bet she'll find him. Better than the bobbies, they say she is."

Bridget smiled. "Well, that's nice to hear. She seems like a very nice lady."

Sadie picked up the beer and one of the gins. "She's the best boss I ever had. You'd never know she was the daughter of an earl. She's not stuck up at all."

Bridget pointed at the second glass of gin. "You going to drink that here?"

"No, I'm taking it over there with me." Sadie nodded at Marlene's table. "I've been waiting to meet this bloke ever since Polly told me he nearly killed Marlene on the coast road. If he *is* a spy, I want to say I met a real one."

"Better be careful," Bridget muttered darkly. "You could be playing with fire. I wouldn't want to see anything happen to you."

Sadie laughed, though a cold finger of apprehension poked her in the gut. Bridget had made the warning sound threatening. She headed for the corner table, hoping fervently that Marlene knew what the heck she was doing.

CHAPTER

❀ 13 ❀

To Sadie's surprise, Bridget followed her over to the table, carrying the second glass of gin.

Marlene looked up as they approached, and her expression wasn't exactly welcoming. When she got a good look at Pete Weston, Sadie could understand why Marlene would want him to herself. The bloke looked like Clark Gable minus his mustache. She put the beer down in front of him and the gin in front of Marlene. "My treat," she announced.

Bridget set the third glass down. "Pete, this is Sadie Buttons. She works at the Manor House."

Pete Weston's polite gaze sharpened with interest. "With Marlene's sister? I say, what fun! Won't you join us?"

"Love to!" Sadie smiled blithely at Marlene's frozen face. "You don't mind, Marl, do you? Oh, by the way, have you met Bridget? She's the new barmaid here."

Marlene set her jaw and glanced at Bridget. "Pleased to meet you, I'm sure."

"Bridget's really livened up the place," Sadie said, taking the seat Pete offered her. "The pub hasn't been the same since she started working here, I'm happy to say. It needed a kick in the arse."

"My sister told me it's a lot more fun down here now," Marlene said, sounding somewhat stilted.

"I do my best." Bridget shoved her fist into the pocket of her apron.

"This place could do with some excitement." Pete gestured at the group of Americans huddled around the dartboard. "Do they give you much trouble, Bridget?"

"Nothing I can't handle."

"I bet the girls like having them around. You must see an awful lot of dillydallying going on."

"I don't have time to notice." Bridget shot a glance at the bar. "Speaking of which, I'd better get back. Looks like Alfie's got his hands full." She took off before Sadie could answer her.

"So what's it like working for the lady of the manor?" Pete asked heartily. "Thanks for the beer, by the way."

"Yes, thank you," Marlene murmured.

"It's hard work." Sadie lifted her glass and took a sip of gin. "I don't mind it, though. Lady Elizabeth is nice and Violet's all right. Martin is a bit of a misery, but then I'd be miserable if I was that old and doddery."

"And that's the only staff up there, right?"

"Except for Desmond, the gardener. Don't see much of him, though. He doesn't come into the house that often."

Pete nodded, and gulped down a mouthful of beer. "What about the Americans? Do you see much of them?"

"Sometimes. Depends how busy they are at the base."

"I expect they run a lot of missions from there."

It was at that moment that Sadie remembered the rumors. Up until then she hadn't really believed that stuff about a spy. It had all seemed so far-fetched. But she'd caught a glimpse of Marlene's face before she'd turned her head, and something in her eyes warned Sadie to keep her mouth shut. "I really couldn't say." She took a large sip of gin before adding, "So where did you say you were from?"

"I didn't. But I live in Surrey." Pete flashed her a killer smile. "What about you, Sadie? Have you got an American boyfriend?"

"No, I ain't."

"Why not? Got something against the GIs?"

Sadie met his gaze steadily over the rim of her glass. "Not really. Have you?"

Pete's laugh didn't quite ring true. "Why would I? I really don't know any of them."

"Pete hasn't been here long enough to meet any Americans," Marlene said, giving Sadie a look that clearly told her to mind her own business.

Unfazed, Sadie beamed at Pete. "Well, I could introduce you to some if you're interested."

"I'm more interested in what you have to say about them. Do you think the village has benefitted from their presence? I mean, look at this place. The GIs must be bringing in money to Sitting Marsh."

"Oh, they bring in money all right," Sadie assured him, forgetting her suspicions again for the moment. "The girls love it, too. 'Course, the older ones are not so keen. They think the Yanks are nothing but trouble. Always fighting with the British blokes, they are, especially the soldiers from the army camp in Beerstowe."

Pete's gaze seemed to penetrate right through her head. "Beerstowe? Where's that?"

"It's about five miles from here. The soldiers sometimes stop off on the way into North Horsham but they don't stay long. Unless they have something going on here. Polly was telling me about a dance they had here at the Town Hall. Almost turned into a massacre. You were there, weren't you, Marl? You must have seen it."

Marlene's face looked like marble. "I don't like talking about it that much."

Alerted once more, Sadie silently cursed her runaway tongue. Fat lot of good she'd be as a spy. She'd spill her guts to the first bloke what smiled at her. "I'd better go." She drained her glass. "I have a Yank waiting to lose some more money at the dartboard."

"Good luck, old girl," Pete murmured. "Thanks for the drink. And the conversation. I thoroughly enjoyed talking to you."

Sadie glanced at Marlene, who looked as if she was about to be sick. "See you later, Marl. I'll be in to get me hair cut next week."

Marlene didn't even answer, and Sadie left the table, wondering if anything she'd said could possibly be useful to an enemy spy.

"You're not saying much," Pete said after Sadie had rejoined the crowd at the dartboard. "Jealous?"

No way was Marlene going to let on that she was jealous of Sadie Buttons. " 'Course not," she said, flicking her hair back from her shoulders. "Why on earth would you think I'd be jealous of *her*?"

Pete glanced at the boisterous young men crowding

around Sadie. "She seems to be having an awfully good
time over there. I must seem pretty dull compared to that
lot."

"Not at all." Marlene smiled at him, then hesitated,
twisting the stem of her glass back and forth in her fingers.
She'd promised herself she wouldn't ask, but now the
question seemed to be burning hot in her brain and she
knew she wouldn't relax until she knew the answer.

Taking a deep breath, she said tentatively, "Pete, do
you mind if I ask you something?"

"Anything, old girl. What is it?"

"Well, I was just wondering . . . I mean . . . you seem
really healthy . . . and you're young and all, and well . . .
I was just wondering . . . why aren't you in the forces?"

The last words had come out in a rush, and seemed to
dangle between them like a string of icicles.

Pete's eyes narrowed and for a moment he looked nothing like the easygoing chap she was beginning to care
about. Then his face cleared and the familiar smile returned. "You surely don't think I'm a deserter or something, do you?"

"Of course not."

She'd said it a bit too quickly, and he chuckled. "Rest
assured, old girl, I'm not on the run from the army or
anything. It's all aboveboard, I promise you."

Feeling only slightly better, Marlene persisted. "You
must have a job, though, don't you? I mean, how do you
make a living?"

"I don't really have to worry about it. The pater makes
gobs of money . . . hands it over whenever I need it. Jolly
good arrangement, if you ask me."

Marlene widened her eyes. "Is he a duke or something?"

"Something." Pete grinned at her. "Stop worrying about

it, darling. Let's just relax and enjoy ourselves. After all, it's wartime. Who knows what's going to happen tomorrow?"

Darling. He'd called her *darling.* All her misgivings vanished at the sound of that one word. Pete was right. Who cared where the money came from, or what he was doing in Sitting Marsh. He was there with her right now, and God only knew how long he'd stay. The best thing she could do for herself was relax and enjoy it, and make the most of every moment. For something told her that Peter Weston wasn't going to be around long enough to worry about anything.

Elizabeth was unprepared for the light tap on her door late that evening. She hadn't expected to see Earl for at least a day or two, since he'd told her he'd be busy at the base. When he poked his head around the door as usual, she was quite sure her flood of happiness was shining all over her face.

"Earl! How wonderful! To what do I owe this unexpected pleasure?"

"You can thank the United States Army Air Force." Earl stepped into the snug warmth of the tiny conservatory and closed the door behind him. "Operations have been suspended again, thanks to this lousy weather."

"Well, I'm happy to hear it. Do sit down." She snatched up a pile of knitting patterns from his chair and dropped them on the table next to her. "Your scotch is in the cocktail cabinet, if you'd like to get it?"

"Thanks, but I think I'll share a glass of your sherry, if that's okay? I'm getting a real taste for the stuff."

"It is rather good, isn't it." She waited for him to fetch a glass from the cabinet, then poured a generous amount for him. "This is so nice. I wanted to talk to you about something and I was afraid it would have to wait for a day or two."

He settled himself in the chair and hooked one knee over the other. "It's always good to see you, Elizabeth. I sure look forward to these times. It's good to sit here with you, chatting over a drink in this cozy room."

She smiled rather wistfully. "Something to remember when you're back in America."

"Something I'll never forget." He raised his glass to her, and the warmth in his eyes did more for her than a dozen glasses of sherry. "Now, what was it you wanted to talk about? I hope George and Gracie haven't been disgracing themselves again?"

Hating to destroy the magic of the moment, she sighed. "The dogs are behaving beautifully. I wanted to talk to you about the painting that Violet brought back from the cottage. I took another look at it last night. I could swear that Mr. Thorncroft painted a submarine in the ocean. I could be wrong, of course, but I'm wondering if he saw something out there and was trying to record it, just in case something happened to him."

"You think he had an idea he could be in danger?"

"I'm not sure." She sent him a troubled look. "There have been rumors going around, Earl. About a German spy suspected of being in the area. I dismissed the idea at first, of course, but now I'm beginning to wonder. George and Sid have been so secretive about this investigation. In fact, I suspect it's the Secret Service who have taken it over. That would sort of suggest that a spy might be involved, don't you think?"

Earl was silent for so long she was worried she'd offended him in some way. Then he put down his glass, and his expression deepened her concern. "I've been agonizing over whether to tell you this or not," he said finally. "It's supposed to be hush-hush."

"I'm sorry, Earl. I don't want to get you into any sort of trouble . . ."

"Elizabeth, there's pretty strong evidence that a spy has been operating in or very close to Sitting Marsh for the past week or so. Maybe much longer. Word is that he's waiting to be picked up off this coastline, probably because it's so isolated. Intelligence interpreted an enemy signal from out to sea, most likely from a submarine. Apparently the guy was supposed to have been picked up a few days ago, but the storms and heavy seas have stopped them from getting in close enough."

Elizabeth sat up straight. "Oh, my! Do your people know where he is?"

Earl shook his head. "I don't know too much about it, since it's supposed to be under wraps, but I guess now that word has gotten out in the village, there's not much point in trying to keep it a secret. If he's still in Sitting Marsh, he probably knows we're on to him by now."

"Then surely he won't wait around to be caught?"

"He may not have any choice if he's waiting to be picked up. In any case, I'd sure like to take a look at that painting of yours."

"Of course. It's in my office. We can go up there right now." She jumped up, knocking the pile of patterns to the floor.

Earl reached forward to pick them up, turning them over in his hand before handing them back to her. "I didn't know you liked to knit."

"I would say just about every woman in England likes to knit. We're taught to do it at an early age."

"Really?" He held the door open for her. "What are you working on?"

"Nothing, yet. I was trying to decide when you came in. I thought it might settle my nerves to sit with some knitting in the evenings."

"Good idea. I take a size thirty-eight chest, if you're interested."

Her laugh was meant to be a light dismissal, but his words had flustered her and it ended in a splutter. She quickly turned it into a cough as she stepped past him and hurried across the library to the hallway.

"I'm not in that much of a rush," Earl said as he caught up with her. "Where's the fire?"

She drew her brows together. "Fire?"

"Never mind. It's an American thing." He grinned at her and, to add to her confusion, took hold of her arm and tucked it under his elbow.

Any contact with him was enough to shatter her composure. Much as she enjoyed it, she couldn't help wondering what Violet would say if she saw the two of them strolling together up the wide staircase to the seclusion of her office.

As they reached the top of the stairs, Elizabeth caught a movement in the shadows of the great hall. Since the blackout, it had been difficult to see anything after dark in the hall, the only lights being placed at either end to brighten the stairways. Consequently, no one visited the area until daylight, when the heavy blackout curtains could be drawn back to let in the sunshine.

Certainly none of her staff should be about at this hour. Violet retired to her room as soon as the supper chores had been taken care of, and both Sadie and Polly were off duty in the evenings. As for Martin, he always went to bed quite early and, in any case, would have trouble finding his way around in the dark.

Nevertheless, Elizabeth was quite sure she'd seen

someone moving around close to where the suit of armor stood. She came to an abrupt halt with a faint gasp of apprehension.

Earl must have heard it nevertheless. He cut off what he was saying and lowered his voice. "What's the matter?"

"Someone's down there," she whispered back.

"You sure?" Earl squinted down the hall. "Maybe it's one of my guys. We'd better take a look. They know this part of the house is off limits to them."

"No . . . wait. It's all right." Elizabeth started forward again, her arm still linked with his. She'd recognized the bowed figure now shuffling toward them. "Martin," she called out sharply. "What are you doing up here at this hour?"

The figure came to an abrupt halt, and a quavery voice echoed eerily down the hall. "Madam? Are you all right?"

"Of course I'm all right."

She could see his face now—a white blob above the dark coat he wore. He started toward them again, his arms working at his sides as he increased his speed to a fast crawl. Again his voice rang out, this time with more urgency.

"Who's there? Who is that with you? Unhand the lady at once, you scoundrel!"

Elizabeth withdrew her arm from Earl's. "It's quite all right, Martin. It's Major Monroe. There's nothing to be alarmed about."

Martin's feet gradually slowed to a stop. "I would venture to say that's entirely a matter of opinion, madam."

"Ouch," Earl muttered beneath his breath.

Embarrassed, Elizabeth said sternly, "Martin, you haven't explained what you are doing here."

"I'm doing my duty, madam." Martin did his best to

straighten his back, grunted, then gave up the attempt. "Someone has to keep watch over the Manor House. There is a war on, you know."

"Yes, I do know, Martin. But I can assure you that we are in no danger. In any case, Major Monroe and his officers are quite capable of protecting us should there be any cause for alarm."

"Really." The disdain in Martin's voice was painfully obvious.

"Perhaps I should leave," Earl said. "I can check out the painting tomorrow."

"You'll do no such thing." Elizabeth glared at her butler, even though he probably couldn't see her in the murky light. "Martin was on his way to bed, weren't you, Martin."

"If you say so, madam. Though I must warn you that your father is most displeased with you. No doubt you shall hear from him in the morning." With a last, baleful glare at Earl, he shuffled past the two of them and made his way slowly down the stairs.

"I thought your father was dead," Earl said as Elizabeth led the way to her office.

"Take no notice of Martin." Elizabeth paused at the door to her office. "He gets confused at times."

"He doesn't like me very much."

"He doesn't know you. In his own inimitable way he's simply trying to protect me. He still thinks of me as the little girl who used to play hide-and-seek with him up and down these hallowed halls."

Earl had his back to the light and she couldn't see his face, but his voice sounded odd when he murmured, "You do have a way of bringing out the protective streak in a man."

She didn't quite know how to answer that, so instead,

she pushed open the office door and flicked on the light switch.

The painting hung on the wall facing them, and she gestured at it as they entered the room. "There it is. Take a look at the shadow in the ocean and tell me what you think it is."

She watched him go up to the painting and study it. Something about the way he stood with his head tilted just a little on one side struck a chord deep inside her. It was one of those moments that she knew would stay with her for a lifetime.

He stood so close. All she had to do was take a step or two toward him and reach for him. She could almost feel the warmth of his body. How she ached to hold him.

Without warning he spun around—too fast for her to wipe the longing from her face. Whatever he was going to say died in the hiss of his breath.

It seemed unnaturally quiet in the room—so quiet she could hear her own heart thudding. Although her head clanged with dire warning, she could not tear her gaze away from his.

It was as if time had ceased to exist, as if the walls had faded away, and they were together in some vast, open valley filled with the warmth and dazzling light of the sun.

Then he took a step toward her, and the spell was broken. In a panic, she remembered all the reasons why this could not happen. The walls came tumbling in again, even as he said, in a voice full of question, "Elizabeth?"

She sidestepped around the desk, unable now to look at him. When she found the strength to speak, she sounded terribly stilted. "So . . . do you think it's a submarine or am I suffering from an overactive imagination?"

He didn't answer her at once. Now she could hear the

relentless ticking of the clock on the wall. She waited, holding her breath, praying he wouldn't say something that would end forever the special friendship that was so imperative to her well-being. Now that she was in danger of losing it, she couldn't bear the thought of the empty days and nights that awaited her.

He spoke at last, and his words did nothing to calm her fears. "There's nothing overactive about your imagination, Elizabeth. Or mine, for that matter. We both know what's going on in our minds. I think it's time we talked about it."

She found it impossible to breathe. Or to speak. She stared hard at the papers lying in front of her—papers that inevitably waited for her attention. In another lifetime, another world, they might be important to her. But not now.

She flinched when he laid both hands on the desk and leaned toward her. "Look at me, Elizabeth. Look at me and tell me you don't know what I'm talking about."

Still she could not look at him. "Earl . . . I . . . can't. *We* can't. It's as simple as that."

She waited, heart pounding, for his response.

After what seemed like a year passing, he straightened. "I think you're right," he said softly. "I think it could very well be a submarine."

CHAPTER

❀ 14 ❀

Marge Gunther never had been one for early rising. She'd grown up on a farm, where her day started just about the time some people were getting home from a late-night party. She'd sworn up and down that once she had her own home, she'd never get up earlier than seven o'clock in the morning.

That meant a mad scramble to get the kids off to school, but it was worth it for the luxury of lying there in her warm bed thinking about all those stupid farmers out there in the rain and the cold wind, with three or four hours of their work day already behind them.

This morning, however, thanks to Sergeant Major Rita Crumm, she'd had to crawl out of her soft feather bed at half past five and get the kids their breakfast and off to school early so she could sit in a wet field with a bunch of other ninnies looking for a so-called spy who hadn't turned up yesterday and wasn't bloody likely to turn up at this hour in the morning, no matter what know-it-all Rita said. So there.

Marge pulled the collar of her raincoat up at the back of her neck, although it was already too late. The rain had seeped down the back of her coat and was busily soaking up the neck of her woolly cardigan. Her knees ached, her stockings were torn, and something had bitten her ear. She could feel it swelling up and beginning to throb.

Spread out on either side of her along the hedgerows were the disgruntled members of the Housewives League. Well, not all of them. Maybe half of them had turned out this morning. Marge wasn't sure why she'd bothered, except she didn't want to be in Rita's bad books. Rita had a way of getting even with people who didn't go along with everything she wanted.

Still, there was a limit to what even Marge would do to keep in Rita's favor. And right now, she was fast approaching that point. In fact, she had almost convinced herself the miserable mess she was in wasn't worth keeping Rita happy, when a movement behind her startled her out of her wits.

She let out a yelp, which she immediately cut off with her hand, slapping herself a bit painfully in the mouth. Annoyed at the cause of her discomfort, she glared at Florrie, who had disobeyed orders to keep several paces apart from the rest and was crouching behind her as if she was about to wet her drawers.

"What are you doing here?" Marge demanded in a hoarse whisper.

"I want to go home."

Marge looked at Florrie's pinched face and felt sorry

for her. The woman was shivering so hard her teeth chattered. "We can't go home. You heard Rita. We have to stay out here until the bird-watcher turns up."

"He's not going to be watching any birds in this weather." Florrie tilted her face to the sodden sky, exposing her cheeks to the rain. "There aren't any blinking birds up there to watch."

Marge sighed. Some people just didn't get it. "He's not watching birds, is he. He's a spy. He's going to be spying."

"What's he spying on?"

"I don't know, do I. That's what we're here to find out. You heard what Rita said. He was out here spying the other morning when we saw him and she thinks he'll be back to do some more spying this morning. Wait a minute." She parted the sprigs of hawthorn and peered through the hole she'd made in the thick hedge. A blank stretch of coast road lay between her and the edge of the cliffs, which were shrouded in a damp fog. "He's not here yet," she muttered.

"No, and he's not coming, neither." Florrie gave a violent shudder. "I think Rita's talking a lot of rot."

"Shsssh!" Marge peered down the line but the soggy mist hid their stalwart leader from view. "Don't you let her hear you say that. She'll have your guts for garters."

"She can have them for all I care. I'm too cold to feel anything anyway."

Marge sighed. "He shouldn't be too much longer anyhow. Then we can all go down to Bessie's and have a nice hot cup of cocoa and a big, fat, hot sausage roll."

Florrie moaned so loud Marge was sure everyone in the line would hear her. "Oo, heck, I'm so hungry me stomach is rattling."

"Your teeth will be rattling if Rita catches you here

with me." Marge peered through her hole again. "Go back to your station and watch for the spy. If he comes by and you're not there, Rita will bury you alive."

"At least it would be warm down there." Florrie started to get up then crouched down again. "What are we supposed to do, anyway, if we see him? Yell to let everyone know he's there? Won't he run away?"

Marge stared at her in disbelief. "Are you daft? Didn't you listen to what Rita told us last night? No, you twerp, you don't yell. You watch him. You watch what he does, then you report back to Rita. You've got to be really, really careful he doesn't see you or hear you."

"Why? If we're going to catch him and take him down to the police station, we'll have to let him know we're here."

"Yes, I know. But we can't catch him until he's done his spying, and he won't do any spying if he knows we're here." Marge shifted her bum on the wet ground and groaned. "So whatever you do, be quiet. Don't make a sound. Just watch him, and if you see him spying, then you creep along the hedge until you get to Rita and you tell her what you saw and she'll tell us what to do next."

"All right."

Florrie started rising to her feet and Marge grabbed her skirt. "Get down, silly. He'll see you if you stand up."

"Marge . . ."

Florrie's voice sounded strange, but Marge didn't want to raise her chin for fear of getting all the rain in her face and down her neck again. "Go back, Florrie," she whispered fiercely.

"Marge . . ."

"For Pete's sake, get back there and watch through your hole."

"Marge, I don't think . . ."

Losing her patience, Marge lifted her chin to glare at

her hapless companion. Only it wasn't Florrie's face she was staring at. It was a man's face, with a long thin pointy nose. Florrie was already scrambling away as fast as she could go, but Marge didn't pay her much attention. She was too busy staring into the face of the man hovering over her.

"Good morning," Alistair Whitton said coldly. "Are you ladies looking for something by any chance?"

Marge didn't wait to answer him. She surged to her feet, tucked her handbag under her arm, and galloped hell for leather out of the field accompanied by six terrified members of the Housewives League.

Polly ducked out of sight as the group of American air men trudged up the stairs to their quarters in the east wing. She'd spent the afternoon working in the office with one ear listening for the arrival of the Jeeps, knowing that Sam Cutter would be among the men returning to the Manor House.

The minute she'd heard the faint roar of the engines, she'd dropped everything and raced along the great hall so that she could be by the stairs as the men trudged up them.

For a few anxious moments she thought that Sam wasn't with them, as one by one they passed by the window where she stood, hidden behind the heavy velvet curtains.

At long last Sam came into view and her heart squeezed at the sight of his weary, scarred face. She resisted the urge to fly up to him and throw her arms around him. Instead, she waited until he'd passed her by, then stepped out behind him. "Why, Sam!" she said cheerfully. "How are you? I ain't . . . haven't seen you in a while."

For an agonizing heartbeat or two she thought he

wasn't going to stop, then he halted and without turning to look at her muttered, "I've been busy."

"So have I." Determined to see this through, in spite of the almost painful pounding of her heart, she stepped around him so that she could face him.

He kept his chin down and she couldn't see his eyes. She wanted to cry, but struggled to control her voice. "It's funny, but me ma was just talking about you this morning. She was wondering how you are and why she hasn't seen you lately."

Sam heaved his bag higher on his shoulder. "You know why she hasn't seen me. I'm surprised she wants to, knowing that I was dating her fifteen-year-old daughter."

"Sixteen," Polly said firmly. "I'm sixteen, Sam. It won't be very long before I'm seventeen."

"Yeah, well, by then I'll either be dead or back in the good old U.S."

Polly's lower lip started trembling and she gritted her teeth to stop it. "Well, anyhow, that's not what I wanted to talk about. Me ma wants you to come to tea next Sunday. I told her I didn't think you'd come, but I said as how I'd ask you, so I'm asking you. Would you please like to come to tea with Ma and me on Sunday afternoon?"

He looked at her then, but there was no warmth in his eyes. "Was this your mom's idea or yours?"

"It was me mum, honest. She knows it weren't your fault we crashed the Jeep. That silly old bloke on a bicycle got in your way, that's all. After all, I didn't get nothing more than a bruise or two and you wouldn't have scraped up your face if you hadn't tried to miss that old man. You saved his life. Everyone knows that."

"I was on the wrong side of the road."

"All the Yanks drive on the wrong side of the road. It's

the right side to you. It weren't your fault, Sam. Nothing was your fault. No one's blaming you."

His hand strayed up to his scarred face and she longed to stroke the battered cheek. "I should've known you weren't twenty," he muttered. "I should've known you were lying to me all that time."

She shuffled her feet, resisting the urge to throw herself on him and beg. "I'm sorry about that, Sam, but it's done now and I can't take it back. Anyhow, I'm not asking you for nothing. I'm just doing what me ma wanted me to and I'm asking you to afternoon tea. If you don't want to come, I'll tell her that."

She turned away, her stomach churning so bad she thought she'd be sick right in front of him.

"No, wait."

She paused, afraid to turn around in case he saw the hope blazing in her eyes.

"Look," he hesitated, then said in a rush, "Okay. If your mom wants me to come, I guess I can make it."

She wiped the smile from her face and made herself speak calmly. Much as she wanted to look at him, she still couldn't trust herself to turn around. "Good. I'll tell her. About four o'clock, all right?"

"I'll be there."

She walked away, even though she knew he still stood there, watching her leave. Sunday. There were too many hours to get through until Sunday. Somehow she'd have to live through them. Somehow.

She waited until she'd turned the corner on the stairs before wrapping her arms around herself in an excited hug. It didn't mean nothing, of course. He was coming to see Ma. But he was coming to tea at her house, and for a little while she'd have a chance to make things up with him.

It wouldn't be easy. If Sadie was right and he was worried about his scars, it could take a long time to get through that wall he'd put up around himself. But as long as there was a shred of hope, she was going to hang in there and do everything she could to make him see how much he really needed her, and how willing she was to be there at his side. Forever.

The rain finally stopped late that afternoon. The winds died down and by the evening the clouds had all but disappeared. Delighted to see the end of the week-long storms, Elizabeth decided to take the dogs for a lengthy, much needed walk. For several days now George and Gracie had been confined to the grounds, and although that afforded them plenty of space, it wasn't quite the same as a brisk run along the cliffs.

Violet, as usual, voiced her concerns as Elizabeth fastened the leads on both dogs in the kitchen. "I don't like the idea of you walking out there on your own. The sun's going down and it'll be dark before you get back. What with murderers and spies running around the village, it's not safe for a woman to be out on her own."

"I'm not going that far." Elizabeth patted the excited dogs on their furry heads. "They need the exercise."

"I still don't see why you can't take them in the morning."

"Because I need the exercise, too. I need fresh air. I need time to think. I have so much going around in my head I can't sleep at night."

"Worrying about that blinking murder, I suppose. I don't know why you can't leave all that stuff up to the proper authorities and spend more time worrying about what's going on here. I've been wasting my breath asking Desmond to prune back those blackberry bushes. He still hasn't done it, and Martin keeps losing his things, or giving them away, I don't know what. He's lost his blinking fountain pen now . . . the one your mother gave him, remember? Good job I have his ration book, or he'd be losing that next."

Elizabeth let herself be dragged to the door by the impatient dogs. "Martin is one of the things I'm concerned about, Violet. I'll give the matter some thought while I'm strolling along the cliffs."

Violet let out a snort of derision. "Stroll? I'd like to see anyone stroll with those two dragging on the lead. Looks like they're the ones taking *you* for a walk, and a fast one at that."

"We'll be back soon, Violet." Thankfully, Elizabeth let the door swing to behind her, and chased up the stairs on the heels of the yapping dogs.

Unfortunately Martin was about to descend as George and Gracie bounded to the top. He ended up in a heap on the floor while Gracie generously cleaned his face with her wet, floppy tongue.

It took several minutes for Elizabeth to restore order and calm the agitated butler enough to allow him to continue on his way. By the time she was finally running down the steps to the driveway, dusk had settled over the grounds.

Happily the clear skies and full moon provided her ample light to find her way to the coast road. Normally she wouldn't have considered walking the dogs that late at night, but after having promised them with one or two of the few words they understood, she hated to disappoint them.

The truth was, she admitted to herself, she really did need this time to herself to sort out the chaos going on in her mind. The brief intimate interlude she'd shared with Earl had shaken her more than she cared to admit.

She had to acknowledge that he knew now how she felt about him. Or at the very least, had a good idea. It was only a matter of time, of course, but she'd hoped to keep that from him for much longer. Indeed, there had been a time when she'd hoped he'd never know, but lately her feelings for him had become difficult to hide. Even Violet seemed to have accepted that there were some things a woman simply couldn't control.

The problem now was what to do about it. How long could she go on resisting the temptation, the way she did last night? How long before Earl did something he would bitterly regret, and hate her for it later? She could understand how hard it was for him, away from home and lonely for a woman's company. Especially with all the terrible dangers he had to face nearly every day. Especially when his own wife didn't seem to be much of a comfort to him.

Nevertheless, the fact remained, he was married. He had a wife and a family. Elizabeth had been through a divorce and knew only too well how people regarded such a scandal. Divorce was something people whispered about, pointed fingers at, and considered a mortal sin. How much worse would their outrage be should she become intimately involved with a married man. In her position, it would be enough to put the entire population of Sitting Marsh against her.

She had an image to uphold. A duty to perform. A tradition to cherish and honor. She could not destroy all that just because she had illicit feelings for a man so far beyond her reach.

So, what was she to do about it?

Right then she felt like screaming her frustration to the

four winds. Instead, she let the dogs off their leads and raced with them along the cliffs until she had no more strength or breath left to keep up with them.

Calling them to heel, she sank onto a wooden bench facing out to sea, and tried not to notice the tangle of barbed wire that obscured her view of the moonlight glimmering on the restless ocean.

Again her thoughts returned to the night before and the moment when she'd thought of nothing but how much she wanted to lean against Earl's broad back. He'd been studying the painting. After those few awkward moments, when she'd steered the conversation back to its proper channels, he'd remarked on the shadowy figure standing in front of the pub in the painting.

After discussing it for several minutes, they had concluded that Basil Thorncroft might very well indeed have been trying to communicate a message. That somehow the submarine, the spy, and the Tudor Arms were all connected.

Earl had even suggested that the figure in the painting could actually be the spy, the very person who had killed the artist. But if so, it was impossible to recognize if the figure was a man or a woman, much less who it might be. In the end, Earl had told her he would discuss the matter with his intelligence officers, and had taken the painting with him.

He'd seemed depressed when he left, as if he knew that things couldn't be the same between them now. Though what either of them planned to do about the situation wasn't even implied.

Which brought her back to the problem with which she'd come out here to wrestle. What *was* she going to do about this whole damn mess?

She stared at the horizon as she struggled for the answer, while the dogs rested panting at her feet. The moon cut a wide silver pathway through the dark sea, which was calm now for the first time in a week. After several minutes of staring and agonizing, she knew that a decision wouldn't be reached that night. She needed time.

She needed to see him again, to gauge how he felt about the whole thing. The best thing she could do for herself, she decided, was go back home and try to sleep. Maybe the morning would bring a clearer mind and with any luck a feasible answer to her problems.

She was about to rise when something caught her eye. A little to the right of the gleaming path of moonlight, a small, bright pinpoint of light glowed out of the darkness, then disappeared. She watched it glow again, vanish, glow, vanish, and glow once more in a distinct pattern.

Excitement caught her breath as she bounced to her feet. There was no doubt about it. The light was some kind of signal far out to sea.

The submarine. Could the Germans be signaling to someone on the shore? If so, who and where?

She peered into the shadowy darkness of the woods that bordered that part of the coast road. The trees were too dense for a light to be seen from there. Unless the spy had climbed a tree. But then he'd have to find the tallest one. No, it made no sense for him to be in the woods. He was either standing on the cliffs, in which case she should be able to see him, or he'd found a more suitable spot from which to signal.

Feverishly she fastened the leads on the dogs and hurried up the coast road toward the manor. There was one place that towered above the village, and any signal from the sea could easily be seen from its windows. The old windmill stood high on the hill, and had been used by the

Home Guard as a lookout during the height of the invasion scare.

Nowadays the Home Guard was busy protecting the cities against Hitler's bombs, more or less leaving the coastal residents to fend for themselves should an invasion actually occur. Which had prompted Rita's formation of the Housewives League—a dubious second best.

Still thinking about Rita and wondering why she hadn't spotted the signals during one of her patrols, Elizabeth paused at the end of the lane that led to the windmill. It would take far too long to walk there. By the time she went back for her motorcycle and rode out, anyone who might be skulking around there would be long gone. Especially when he heard the rattling roar of her ailing engine.

Torn by indecision, she was startled out of her thoughts by a faint sound in the tree close by to where she stood. George barked, and Gracie answered him.

Elizabeth shushed the dogs, and strained her ears to listen. The faint, pitiful meow of a cat called again from the tree. Uttering a soft sound of sympathy, Elizabeth hurried over to the tree and peered up into the branches. It took a moment or two, but finally she spied the dark silhouette of the cat against the moonlight filtering through the branches.

She called to it, and the cat answered her with a mournful yowl. Elizabeth studied the trunk of the tree. There were a few sturdy-looking branches within reach. It really didn't look that difficult a climb. She simply couldn't go home and leave the poor thing stranded up there. She wouldn't have a wink of sleep worrying about it.

She ordered the dogs to sit, then hitched up her skirt. At the same moment, George uttered a deep growl in his throat. The cat responded with a ferocious hiss.

"Be quiet, George," Elizabeth muttered as she reached for the first branch.

Gracie's growl sounded louder, and much more urgent. George bared his teeth and growled even louder. Elizabeth froze. They weren't growling at the cat, after all. They'd heard what she could now hear. Footsteps echoing in the darkness behind her. Footsteps that were rapidly drawing closer.

CHAPTER

❀ 15 ❀

Elizabeth laid a hand on each dog's head, and peered down the coast road to where the shadowy figure of a man strode toward her. A leather strap swung from his shoulder . . . binoculars by the look of it. She couldn't see his face beneath the brim of the trilby hat he wore pulled down low over his forehead.

Both dogs were bristling now, a ridge of hair raised like furry hillocks down the middle of their backs. Bravely they faced the intruder, bodies trembling in anticipation.

Sensing their alarm, Elizabeth fastened a finger under each straining collar and forced a note of authority in her voice. "Who's there?"

The man stopped, as if he'd heard them for the first

time, then after a second, continued heading toward them. The rumbling growls grew louder.

Then his voice drifted out of the darkness. "Lady Elizabeth? Is that you?"

Still on guard, she watched him approach, while she murmured words of comfort to quiet the dogs. He halted a few steps away and took off his hat, giving her a little nod of recognition.

"Good evening, Mr. Whitton." She was proud of the calm note in her voice, even though George continued to growl low in his throat. "What brings you out here this time of night?"

"I was about to ask you the same thing, your ladyship." Alistair Whitton looked as if he might stretch out a hand toward the dogs, then changed his mind. "It's rather late for a lady to be walking the cliffs alone."

She couldn't decide if the odd note she'd heard in his voice was disapproval or something more sinister. She was beginning to wish she hadn't obeyed the impulse to bring the dogs out to the lonely coast road after dark. Perhaps Violet had been right, after all. Maybe it hadn't been such a good idea.

"I'm not alone, as you can see." She jerked George's lead and he growled again. She was pleased to see the bird-watcher take a step backward. "I have ample protection," she added for good measure.

"Very wise. One never knows what might be lying in wait in the dark these days. It pays to be extra careful."

"Quite. These are dangerous times." As if agreeing with her, a dismal yowl echoed behind her.

Alistair Whitton seemed startled. "What was that?"

"It's a cat stranded in a tree, poor thing." Elizabeth released the dogs' collars but kept a firm hold on their leads. "Actually, I'm awfully glad you came along. It's not very high up. With your height you should be able to reach it without climbing too high."

"Climbing?" The bird-watcher's voice actually rose to a falsetto. "I couldn't possibly climb that tree."

"You wouldn't have to climb very far. No more than six or eight feet, I should think."

Alistair Whitton shuddered. "There has to be another way. In fact . . ."

To Elizabeth's horror, he stooped and picked up a sizable pebble. Before she could protest, he drew back his arm and let fly. A second later the cat shrieked, hissed, then streaked down the tree and off into the darkness.

"There," Alistair Whitton muttered, "that takes care of that. I've always hated cats, anyway. They eat birds, you know."

Elizabeth watched him dust off his hands and for a moment was tempted to set the dogs on him. "It's in a cat's nature to chase birds. They are hunting for prey. Just as some people hunt foxes and deer."

Alistair Whitton gave her an unpleasant look. "Usually wealthy people who have nothing better to do with their time."

If that was a dig at her, it was totally wasted, Elizabeth thought wryly. She looked beyond him, to where the ocean heaved beneath the bright moon. She could no longer see the light flickering out at sea. Either the men on the submarine—if it was, indeed, a submarine—had given up or they'd received the signal they'd been expecting. In either case, it was too late to do anything about it now.

"Well," the bird-watcher muttered, "I'm in rather a hurry, so I'll bid you good night, Lady Elizabeth."

She studied him for a moment. "It's a little late to be observing birds, isn't it?" She gestured at the field glasses hanging from his shoulder. "You can't see much in the dark with those, I shouldn't think."

It might have been her imagination, but Alistair Whitton's shrewd eyes seemed to turn a little glassy. "It depends on what one is looking at." He glanced up at the sky. "This is the first clear night I've had since I arrived. I thought I'd take advantage of it. I've been wanting to observe the night owl I've heard hooting in the woods these past few nights. I should be able to spot its eyes with the help of the moonlight."

"Perhaps." She stared pointedly past him at the thick line of trees beyond. "Aren't you going the wrong way?"

"Am I?" His glaze flicked to the lane. "I thought I'd make for the hill above the woods. I can get a better focus on where the owl might be from up there."

"In that case, don't let me keep you. I'm sure you're anxious to follow up on your quest."

"Quite, quite. Well, I'll say good night, then." He crossed the road to the lane, then paused to look back at her. "Enjoy your walk, your ladyship."

She had the feeling he was waiting for her to leave. Which was exactly what she intended to do. There was nothing more she could do here. The best thing she could do was find Earl and tell him what she'd seen. He'd know what to do next.

With that in mind, she trotted back to the manor at a steady pace, her heart racing with the exertion. At least, that's what she told herself, rather than admit that the thought of seeing Earl again now that her feelings had been exposed was enough to stop her heart beating altogether.

The lonely hoot of an owl echoed across the dark woods as Alistair Whitton trudged up the lane. He quickened his pace, certain that he had located his quarry in the clearing at the top of the hill. The windmill loomed up ahead—a ghostly silhouette against the night sky, its battered and broken arms frozen by decay.

Beyond it, the line of trees stretched all the way down to the coast road. He'd walked for miles, moving in a circle, rather than risk the dark depths of the woods at night. Now he was almost there. His patience had finally paid off.

He hurried past the towering walls of the windmill, his gaze fixed on the clearing. Any minute now he expected to see the small yellow gleam of light that would lead him to his target.

He was several paces away from the windmill when he heard the soft fluttering sound. He paused, anxious to go on, yet curious about what he'd heard. It could be a bat, in which case he'd do well to leave it alone. On the other hand, it could be something else. Something that he'd been on the lookout for ever since he'd arrived in Sitting Marsh.

He turned back and surveyed the windmill. The door looked frail enough. Making up his mind, he retraced his steps and approached with caution. To his surprise, the door was unlocked, and swung in easily at his touch. He waited, listening for the sound again, but now all was silent.

Perhaps he'd imagined it after all. He was about to turn away when a soft scuffling disturbed the quiet depths. Curiosity got the better of him after all. Leaving the door open to allow the pale moonlight to spill inside, he stepped across the threshold of the creaking, musty windmill.

• • •

Elizabeth was quite breathless when she arrived back at the Manor House. She almost bowled poor Martin over when, in her haste to find Earl, she pushed the door open the second the feeble butler had begun to pull on it.

Luckily she heard him cry out, and refrained from pushing any farther until the crack was wide enough for her to slip through. The dogs bounded in with her, and Martin's querulous voice called out after her as she hurried up the stairs.

"Not now, Martin," she called back. "I'm in a dreadful hurry." Heedless of the dogs bounding joyfully at her side in the forbidden territory of the great hall, Elizabeth ran to the other end, her feet making no sound on the plush carpet.

All was quiet as she reached the east wing. The officers were apparently either at the base or pursuing other interests in town. After rapping on the door of Earl's room several times to no avail, she hurried back to her office and put in a call to the base.

Earl had left some time ago, she was told by the stern voice of the officer who answered her. Replacing the receiver, she tried to decide what to do next. Having seen the signal for herself, clearly her duty was to notify the authorities. Which meant calling in the local constables. Who, in turn, would have to notify whoever was in charge of the case, since it was supposedly out of their hands.

In any case, it seemed unlikely that they would be able to do anything about it that night. The submarine had apparently finished its signaling and left. Assuming, of course, that it was the submarine.

Elizabeth sighed. Having been caught in similar situations before, she knew the dangers of assuming anything. Which was why it would be unwise to imagine that Alistair Whitton had anything to do with those mysterious signals flickering out at sea.

Yet the bird-watcher had been acting peculiar, to say the least. Could it be merely a coincidence that he was out there on the cliffs, with his field glasses, after dark, at the precise time an enemy submarine was possibly signaling to the shore?

More assumptions. Dare she raise a hue and cry, knowing it could well be a false alarm? Then again, could she simply ignore what she'd seen and risk allowing an enemy spy to escape, possibly with devastating information about the Allied bombing missions?

If only Earl were there. He'd know the best thing to do. Where was he, anyway?

Doing her best to curb her irritation, she chided herself. It was none of her business where Earl had gone. The best thing she could do for herself was go down to the conservatory and pour a generous glass of sherry. It would help calm her nerves.

The dogs were anxious to leave the confines of her office, and she ushered them outside and closed the door. She was almost at the bottom of the stairs with them when she heard the faint growl of a Jeep's engine coming up the driveway. Both dogs pricked up their ears and looked at her expectantly, their tails beginning to flick back and forth.

How they could tell which Jeep Earl was driving would always be a mystery to her. When she'd mentioned as much to Violet, the housekeeper had scoffed, saying the dogs welcomed anything that moved. But Elizabeth knew better. George and Gracie had an instinct when it came to Earl, and they knew when he was near.

She ran with them to the front door, and feverishly pulled back the heavy bolts that secured it. When she lifted the final latch and pulled the door open, the dogs raced through the opening then bounded down the steps and across the courtyard.

The Jeep came to an abrupt halt as they dashed into the beams of the headlights, and an irritable male voice uttered a very American curse.

Her excitement at seeing him again was tinged with apprehension as she flew down the steps to join the ecstatic animals. She watched Earl climb out of the Jeep, shaking his head.

"One of these days I'm gonna run right over these idiots." He squatted down and allowed the delighted dogs to greet him with their wet tongues. "What are they doing outside this time of night?"

"I let them out." Relief made her heady. His voice had sounded perfectly normal, and she could see no tension or wariness in his face when he looked at her. It was going to be all right, after all. All her worrying had been unnecessary. She pushed Gracie's eager head away from him as he climbed to his feet. "We've had quite an exciting night."

Earl's voice sharpened. "What's happened?"

She told him, in breathless, broken sentences in her haste to get it all out. "I can't really say that Alistair Whitton was doing anything wrong, of course, but he certainly was acting very strangely, and he wasn't at all pleased to see me there. I just hate to think that if he *is* the spy, he might escape. Do you think I should report it? After all, I can't say for sure that it was a submarine or anything, but—"

Earl's hand descended on her shoulder, effectively cutting off the rest of her sentence. "The first thing you've gotta do is relax. Everything's under control. The lights you saw could have been from a patrol boat. I heard that

one has been patrolling the shoreline ever since the first
signals were detected. If there was a U-boat out there
tonight, I think they'd know it."

"Oh." Now she felt foolish. "So Alistair Whitton could
be on the trail of a night owl, after all."

"Could well be, I guess."

"Drat! I thought I'd solved the whole murder thing."

His expression seemed quizzical in the moonlight.
"You thought the bird-watcher killed Thorncroft?"

"Well, I thought he might have. After all, it seems
pretty obvious that Basil Thorncroft was trying to tell us
something with that painting, which means he must have
had some suspicions about who the spy might be. Which
was most likely why he was killed, don't you think? What
I don't understand is why he put it all in a painting, instead of reporting what he knew to the authorities."

The pressure of Earl's hand guided her back toward the
front steps of the manor, his arm draped around her shoulders. "Maybe he didn't know as much as the killer thought
he knew. He could have been playing with ideas, and just
happened to hit on the truth. Then again, we don't know
for sure that's why he was killed."

"Well, George more or less confirmed it. It's the most
logical reason. I believe the killer must have seen the
painting and recognized himself. At least enough to war-
rant silencing Mr. Thorncroft permanently."

"I don't see how when the face is too blurry to make
out."

"Well, there could be something about it that's familiar
enough to make it worth killing someone. After all, if the
spy was forced by the weather to wait until his friends
could come into shore to pick him up, he couldn't risk
anyone being remotely suspicious of him before he had a
chance to escape."

Earl paused at the front door, his gaze on the sky. "Well, the weather seems to have changed now. If he's going to escape by sea, now would be the time to do it."

Elizabeth caught her breath. "You think he'll try tonight?"

"Depends on if he knows about the patrols or not. My guess is that they won't come in to pick him up and risk getting caught. If it were me, I'd find another way to get him out of here."

"Then we have to find out who he is before he has a chance to do that." She pushed the door open and stepped into the hall, the dogs sweeping past her to race for the kitchen steps. "I think I'd like a night cap. Would you care to join me?"

He pushed his cuff back and stared at his watch. "It will have to be a quick one. I've got some paperwork I have to catch up on."

"I'll just shut the dogs in the kitchen and then we can go to the conservatory."

He waited while she ran down the back stairs to settle the dogs for the night, then followed her to the conservatory, where he poured them both a drink.

Nursing her sherry in both hands, Elizabeth brooded over her meeting with the enigmatic bird-watcher. When the silence had gone on a little too long, she announced somewhat defiantly, "I can't rest until I've found out who killed Basil Thorncroft."

"Elizabeth—"

She held up her hand. "I know what you're going to say, but save your breath. That man was a tenant in one of my cottages, and I can't just sit here while his murderer plans his getaway."

Earl's skepticism showed clearly on his face. "So what do you plan to do?"

She thought for a long moment. "So far there are two possible suspects. The way I see it, Basil Thorncroft painted the Tudor Arms in the wrong place to draw attention to it. He put a figure in front of it, waving to a submarine in the ocean. I think he was trying to tell us that the person he suspected of being a spy was staying at the Tudor Arms. There are three men staying there who are strangers to the village. Both of them were on the cliffs the morning of the murder around the time Mr. Thorncroft was killed."

"How do you know what time he was killed?"

"Dr. Sheridan told me he probably died two to four hours before we discovered him. That puts the time of death between six and eight o'clock. Rita Crumm and her housewives met Alistair Whitton on the cliffs shortly after eight, and Marlene met Peter Weston shortly before. Either one of them could have just come from the cottage."

"What about the guy next door? Captain Carbunkle?"

Elizabeth frowned. "Yes, I have to admit that's odd. Perhaps I should talk to Priscilla. Bridget told me that she and Wally are very close. I must say that surprised me. I had no idea they even knew each other that well, much less keeping company."

"Guess you don't know everything that goes on in Sitting Marsh."

She gave him a coy look. "Sooner or later I find out. In fact, the only one person I haven't met yet is Peter Weston. I plan to remedy that tomorrow."

"I don't like the thought of you messing with this on your own, Elizabeth. It could be real dangerous. Why don't you talk to the constables about all this and let them handle it."

"Because it won't do any good. It's out of their hands anyway, and they'll just tell me to stay out of it. If I'm going to find out who killed Basil Thorncroft, I have to do this on my own."

He uttered a heartfelt groan. "That's usually when you end up in trouble."

"I'll be careful, Earl. You'll see. I've learned my lesson and I won't do anything silly this time. I'm just going to ask a few questions, that's all."

"Promise?"

She smiled at him with affection. "I promise."

He seemed vaguely reassured by that. She sat for several moments, thinking hard, until he said with a hint of apprehension, "What are you turning over in that devious mind now?"

She hesitated before answering him. "It's nothing," she said finally. "At least, I don't think it's anything. Now and again, when I get involved in a murder case, I get the feeling that I know something important—something I can't quite grasp. I have that feeling now. That somewhere in my mind I know the answer to all this. I just wish I knew what it was."

Shaking his head, Earl drained his glass, and much to her dismay, rose to his feet. "You know what I think? I think we both need some sleep. I'm going to leave you alone so you can rest. Maybe you'll wake up in the morning with all the answers."

She glanced up at him out of the corner of her eye. "You think I'm nutty, don't you."

He laughed out loud—a sound that never failed to thrill her. "I think you are an intelligent, compassionate woman who has a genuine desire to fulfill what she considers her duty to the people of Sitting Marsh. Who, by the way, are real fortunate to have her loyalty."

"Thank you. But you also think I'm eccentric."

"Aren't most of the British considered eccentric?"

She wrinkled her nose. "Are we? I suppose some of us might be. Certainly not all of us."

She stood, and he rested both hands on her shoulders for a moment. "Eccentric or not, I think you are charming. If a little misguided and a tad reckless. Promise me again that you won't do anything foolish."

"I won't attempt to apprehend a murderer single-handedly, if that's what you mean."

"That most certainly is what I mean." He smiled down at her. Though his eyes mirrored his concern. "Good night, Elizabeth. Sleep well."

The echo of his voice and the memory of the warmth in his face stayed with her through most of the night.

It was with considerable shock that she heard the news the next morning. Violet greeted her at the kitchen door with a grave face and words she found hard to comprehend.

"They found Alistair Whitton this morning," Violet said bluntly. "He was at the foot of the old windmill. Broke his neck. He's dead."

CHAPTER

❧ 16 ❧

"I can't believe it." Elizabeth sat down heavily on the kitchen chair. "I was just talking to him last night. What happened? Who found him?"

"Marge Gunther's kids, on their way to school. They told their teacher when they got to the classroom, and she called the constables. I just got off the telephone with Marge a little while ago. She's that upset, you'd think it was her kids lying there instead of a bird-watcher who nobody knows."

Elizabeth watched Violet vigorously stir the porridge steaming on the stove and tried to make sense of what she'd just heard. "Did Marge know how it happened?"

Violet stopped stirring and turned off the gas under the heavy pot. "George says he must have leaned out the win-

dow to look at a bird's nest or something. His field glasses
were caught on a nail up there. He must have lost his
balance and fell, poor bugger. Never could understand
why those people took such risks with their lives just to
look at a bird's nest."

. "George found Mr. Whitton's field glasses hanging
from the window? But that's at the top of the windmill.
It has to be at least sixty feet from the ground."

"Which could explain," Violet said dryly, "how he
broke his neck when he fell out of it."

Elizabeth rose sharply to her feet. "Don't serve porridge
for me, Violet. I'll get something from Bessie's Bake
Shop later."

Violet's eyebrows shot up her forehead. "What? But I
cooked a whole pot of it. What am I supposed to do with
it?"

"Give it to Martin, he'll eat it." Elizabeth paused at the
door. "Where is he, by the way? He's usually sitting here
waiting for his breakfast by now."

"Gawd knows where he is." Violet put the lid on the
pot and wiped her hands on her apron. "Must be sleeping
late or something. I'll go and knock on his door." She
tilted her head on one side like an inquisitive sparrow.
"Where are you going in such a hurry, anyway?"

"To talk to George. And a few other people."

"He won't tell you nothing. Marge said he was being
very mysterious about the whole thing. She thinks that the
bird-watcher was a spy, and fell out the window while he
was trying to look for signals out at sea. 'Course, when
she told George that, Marge said he laughed and told her
she was imagining things."

"Well, I don't know if Mr. Whitton was a spy or not."
Elizabeth opened the kitchen door and looked back at Violet. "But I don't think he fell out of that window."

Violet stared at her. "You don't? Why not?"

"Just a hunch." Elizabeth left before Violet could re-
spond to that and hurried up the steps to the front door.
She needed to talk to George before tackling anyone else
that day. If what she suspected was true, then she needed
to warn Marlene about her remaining suspect, Peter Weston. And as soon as possible.

She had to stop for petrol on her way to the High Street
and it took longer than she liked. Having missed breakfast, her stomach was growling, especially when she'd
smelled the fragrance of newly baked bread as she passed
Bessie's shop. There was nothing in the world like that
smell, she thought as she climbed off her motorcycle with
as much decorum as was possible.

After removing her scarf, she straightened the straw hat
it had anchored and marched into the front office of the
police station. The stench in there quickly dulled her appetite. The building had once housed horses for a local
hostelry in the days before the motorcar, and Elizabeth
was convinced the odor of horse manure still permeated
the walls. How George and Sid tolerated it day after day
she would never understand, unless their senses had become immune to it.

George, as usual, sat behind the desk, ponderously
scribbling in a notepad with a bitten pencil that he kept
returning to his mouth to moisten with his tongue. His
expression when Elizabeth greeted him was not exactly
welcoming.

"Your ladyship? What can I do for you this fine morning?"

"You can tell me what happened to Alistair Whitton,"
Elizabeth said briskly.

The closed expression she'd anticipated appeared on his

face. "Accident," he said briefly. "Broke his neck in a fall."

"From where?"

"From the window of the old mill." He scratched his balding head with the pencil. "I'm surprised you didn't know that, m'm. The news is all over the village."

"Well, it is what I heard." Elizabeth sat herself down on the chair in front of him. "But I'm having a little trouble believing it."

George's sigh suggested he had the troubles of the world sitting on his frail shoulders. "Oh, and why's that, your ladyship?"

"Because Alistair Whitton was afraid of heights. He never would have climbed those rickety stairs, much less leaned out of that window, unless it was a matter of life and death."

George stared at her for a full five seconds before answering. "How do you know he was afraid of heights?"

"He told me, when I warned him about straying too close to the edge of the cliffs. What's more, when I asked him to climb a tree last night to rescue a cat, he visibly shuddered at the thought."

"You saw him last night?" George frowned. "I thought he'd died before that. What was he doing in the windmill after dark?"

"Exactly."

"He was afraid of climbing a tree? Bit of a ninny, wasn't he?"

"He didn't strike me as a coward, George. Just a man with a phobia. Lots of people are afraid of heights."

"Then why did he climb to the top of the windmill?"

"He might have had no choice."

George's eyes narrowed. "What exactly are you getting at, your ladyship?"

"I think," Elizabeth said calmly, "that either Mr. Whitton was a spy and was trying to signal to someone at sea—"

"That's utter nonsense." George cleared his throat. "If you'll pardon me, your ladyship, but—"

"Or," Elizabeth went on doggedly, "he ventured into the windmill for some reason and saw someone or something he shouldn't have seen."

George began blustering, a sure sign he was rattled. "Now wait a minute, your ladyship, if you're saying this wasn't an accident, well, all I can say is . . ." His words trailed off.

"Yes?"

"Nothing. I can't say anything at all."

"I didn't think so." Elizabeth rose to her feet. "George, if you won't tell me what's going on, I'll have to find out my way. And you know how much trouble that can be for you. Your inspector is already upset with you, is he not?"

George visibly paled. "Lady Elizabeth, I beg you—"

"We're wasting time, George. There's a spy somewhere in this village and he could escape at any time. That's why Basil Thorncroft was killed, wasn't it?"

George gave her a tight nod of his head.

"Because he knew the identity of the spy?"

"They think so."

"Who's they? The Secret Service?"

George looked as if he would be sick right in front of her. "Lady Elizabeth—"

"Who do they think might be the spy?"

He finally gave up. "They don't know yet, as far as I know. All they know is that he might have killed one of their agents and—"

Elizabeth gasped. "Basil Thorncroft was a secret agent?"

George's face flamed. "I didn't tell you that."

"Yes, you did," Sid's voice said helpfully from the back room.

"George, do they have any suspects?" Elizabeth leaned her palms on the desk. "What about Peter Weston? Have they talked to him?"

"I don't know." George lifted his hands in appeal. "Honest, your ladyship, I don't know anything more than that. They told us to stay out of it."

"Well, you'd better tell them to search that windmill pretty thoroughly. I believe that our resident spy is not only responsible for Mr. Thorncroft's death, he killed Mr. Whitton as well. Meanwhile, I have to talk to Marlene." Elizabeth marched to the door, then looked back at him. "Don't let him get away, George. No matter who or what Mr. Thorncroft might have been, he was my tenant. In my cottage. And now two people have died in Sitting Marsh. Someone has to pay for that." .

She left, one thought on her mind now. To warn Marlene.

Luckily, there was only one customer in the little hairdresser's shop when Elizabeth entered a few minutes later. The other two girls were in the back room, laughing and chatting over fragrant-smelling coffee. Elizabeth's stomach rumbled as she greeted Marlene.

"I'll be with you in a moment, your ladyship," Marlene called out as the door jangled closed behind Elizabeth. Did you want to make an appointment?"

Elizabeth waved her hand in dismissal. "No, it's all right, Marlene. I just wanted a quick word with you when you can spare me a minute."

"Right ho, your ladyship. I just have to put Priscilla under the dryer and—"

Elizabeth uttered an exclamation as a familiar head emerged from the sink. "Priscilla! How fortunate. I wanted to talk to you as well. This will save me a trip."

Priscilla Pierce, a small, jittery woman with dark eyes that never seemed to sit still, fluttered her long fingers in front of her mouth. Her gray hair clung in wet strands to her gaunt face, making her cheekbones look even more skeletal than normal. "Oh, Lady Elizabeth," she said, in a voice that sounded as if she'd just climbed Mount Everest, "whatever could you want with me?"

Marlene was staring at her with frank curiosity in her face. Caught off guard, Elizabeth said quickly, "I was planning on going to Bessie's Bake Shop for a late breakfast. Perhaps you'd like to join me, Priscilla?"

The poor woman looked positively terrified. "Oh, m'm, I'm terribly sorry, but I already ate breakfast."

Elizabeth did her best to calm her with a smile. "A cup of tea then? Bessie makes the most divine Chelsea buns. All that wonderful icing and delicious cinnamon filling. It makes me quite faint to think about it."

To her alarm, Priscilla looked as if she might, indeed, faint dead away. "Th . . . thank you, m'm. That would be very nice, I'm sure."

"Right," Marlene said brightly. "Under the dryer with you. We'll make you look beautiful for your visit to Bessie's."

Considering the woman usually wore her hair snagged in a hairnet, that would be a minor miracle, Elizabeth thought, then chided herself for being uncharitable.

She watched Marlene settle Priscilla under the dryer, and waited for the girl to join her in the foyer. Marlene looked apprehensive as she seated herself on one of the chairs.

"It's not me dad, is it?" she asked as Elizabeth inwardly rehearsed what she had to say.

"No, no, of course not," Elizabeth hurried to reassure her. "This has nothing to do with any of your family. I wanted to talk to you about Peter Weston."

"Oh." Marlene's face crumpled and for a moment Elizabeth was certain she was about to burst into tears.

"My dear," she said quickly. "What's happened? He didn't hurt you, did he?"

Marlene shook her head and fumbled in her apron pocket for a handkerchief. She dabbed carefully at her eyes then blew her nose. "No, m'm. Not in the way you think. It's just that I thought he was such a nice bloke, and he turned out to be a blinking liar!" The last word came out on a wail.

"Oh, dear." Elizabeth's pulse quickened with expectation. "What did he lie about?"

"Well, your ladyship . . ." Marlene sniffed, then went on somewhat tearfully. "He wouldn't tell me nothing about himself, except his family was well off, which was probably another lie. Anyway, he kept asking all these questions. Not just me, but everyone we met. It made me nervous, so I told him I wasn't going out with him again until he told me why he was in Sitting Marsh."

"I see." Elizabeth waited, and when Marlene went on sniffing without any sign of continuing, she prompted gently, "He told you?"

Marlene gave her an unhappy nod. "Yes, your ladyship. He told me he's a newspaper reporter. He was down here in the village because it's near the American base, and he's doing a story on how the English people react to the

Yanks being in town. That's why he was asking all them questions."

Elizabeth studied her face. "And you believe him?"

"Yes, m'm. I didn't at first, but he showed me his reporter's card with his picture on it, and pictures of him in the newspaper office and newspaper stories with his name on them. That's why he's not in the army. Because of his job. He said he didn't tell me at first because he thought no one would talk to him if they knew he was a reporter, and then he didn't tell me later because he was afraid I'd think that's why he was taking me out . . . to find out about the Yanks." She sniffed again. "I know that's why he did take me out. It's the only thing he did lie about."

Elizabeth let out her breath in a sigh of frustration. "Where is he now? At the Tudor Arms? I'd like to talk to him."

Marlene's face puckered again. "You can't, m'm. Not unless you go to London to talk to him. He left yesterday. Said he had to get back to file his story."

"You saw him leave?"

"Yes, m'm. I saw him off, even though I knew it was all a lie . . . all those nice things he said to me." A tear finally squeezed out of her eye and down her cheek. "I do miss him, though."

"I'm sure you do." Elizabeth leaned forward and patted her hand. "He'll be back, no doubt. And if not, you'll know it wasn't meant to be and that there's someone even better waiting for you somewhere."

"Yes, m'm. When I think how he nearly killed me the first time we met, I should have known then it weren't meant to be." Marlene attempted a smile, but Elizabeth could tell she didn't have her heart in it. She felt sorry for the girl, and for herself.

She'd been so sure that Peter Weston was responsible

for the two deaths in Sitting Marsh that week. But if he'd left town yesterday, he couldn't have attacked Mr. Whitton, and it didn't seem as if he could be a spy after all. Now it seemed as if she was left with only one unanswered question. Maybe two. Where was Captain Carbunkle the night of the first murder and, perhaps even more importantly, the night of the second.

To Violet's surprise and concern, Martin was not in his room when she tapped on the door that morning. After peering into the room to make quite sure he wasn't still asleep, she sent Sadie to the drawing room and library to look for him, while she took it upon herself to go up the stairs to the great hall. This time, if Martin was up there talking to a suit of armor, she wanted to see him do it.

The moment she reached the top of the stairs, she saw the old fogey. He was standing in front of the armor all right, talking earnestly away as if that pile of scrap iron could hear him.

Violet had never liked that suit of armor. Gave her the creeps, it did. Staring at her with its invisible eyes, like it was watching her every move. It was all very well for the master to tell her there was no skeleton inside it. She couldn't help it if her mind kept imagining a dead knight inside. Maybe his spirit still lurked there, watching her, waiting . . .

Violet shuddered, and shook the silly ideas out of her head. She was getting as bad as Martin, imagining ghosts and spirits in the great hall. It was all the portraits hanging on the wall, that was the trouble. All those ancient ancestors, whose eyes really did watch her as she scurried down the long hall.

Her feet made no sound on the soft carpet, and she'd almost reached Martin when he lifted a trembling hand

and snapped back the visor on the knight's helmet. She saw something in his hand—something small and square with a glint of silver in the sunlight that poured through the tall window.

She stopped short, waiting to see what the old goat did with it. To her utter astonishment, Martin pushed the object through the visor and let it fall. It bumped and clattered inside all the way down to the feet, then came to rest. Martin stood back, gave a little bow, and said, "You have done your duty well. I shall return."

"What in the blue blazes do you think you are doing?" Violet demanded.

Martin seemed to leap a few inches off the floor and staggered backward, clutching his jacket in the region of his heart. He stood gasping for air, while Violet wondered guiltily if this time she'd gone too far and scared the old boy into a heart attack.

She was about to go to him when he said, in a surprisingly strong voice, "Do you have to bellow in my ear like a frustrated bull? You made me bite my tongue."

"Too bad you don't do that more often." She advanced on him, reassured by the high spots of color in his cheeks. "What did you put inside that armor? That's what I want to know."

"None of your damn business."

"Perhaps madam will think it's her business."

Martin glared at her over the rims of his glasses. "There's no need to bother madam with this. I'm perfectly capable of handling things myself."

Violet tilted her head on one side. "Handle what?"

"The guard duty, of course. We have to keep guard against the enemy."

"What enemy would that be, then?"

Martin sniffed. "You're a woman. You wouldn't understand."

Violet thinned her lips. "I understand that you are damaging a very valuable antique. Madam would not be happy to hear that."

"Damage? Good Lord, woman, I'm not damaging him. I'm paying him."

"Paying him?"

"Yes, to keep guard of the great hall." He raised his hand to shield his mouth from the suit of armor. "They won't do it for free, you know."

Understanding dawned as Violet stared at him. "Is *that* where your watch, and whalebone, and pen have gone? Down the armor's guts?"

Martin winced. "I say, Violet, you don't have to put it quite so crudely."

She shook her head, wondering what Lizzie was going to say when she heard this. Then again, maybe she should keep quiet about it for now. After all, Lizzie had enough on her mind, what with all this stuff about a spy and people dying all over the place.

"Come on, you silly old goat," she told Martin. "Your breakfast is getting cold." She left him to follow her down the stairs, wondering whom she should worry about the most—Martin with his delusions or Lizzie with her dangerous habit of getting involved in murder. Then again, there was still this little matter of Beatrice Carr and the raffle tickets. Sooner or later she'd get to the bottom of that, too. It was just a matter of time.

CHAPTER
❀ 17 ❀

Elizabeth waited until Bessie had served her and Priscilla with buns and a steaming pot of tea before broaching the subject uppermost in her mind. "I'm a little concerned about Captain Carbunkle," she said, coming straight to the point. "He's behaving rather strangely. I do hope he's not ill."

Priscilla dropped her teaspoon on her saucer with a loud clatter. "Captain . . . er . . . Carbunkle, your ladyship?"

"Yes." Elizabeth fixed a stern eye on Priscilla's pinched face. "I understand that you and he are quite close."

Priscilla's face turned a light shade of purple. "Excuse m-me, m'm, but I'd like to know who told you that."

Elizabeth raised a delicate eyebrow. "Is it not true, then?"

"Oh, dear." Priscilla's gaze searched desperately around the room as if looking for help. When she realized none was forthcoming, she picked up her spoon, stirred her tea, and replaced the spoon carefully in the saucer. "The captain and I are friends, yes," she said cautiously.

"More than friends," Elizabeth suggested firmly. "I understand that Wally spends a good deal of time at the Tudor Arms while you are playing the piano for the song night."

Priscilla violently nodded her head. "Yes, he does, but that doesn't mean—"

"For instance . . . last Sunday night?"

"L-Last Sunday?"

"Yes. Wasn't the captain with you at the Tudor Arms?"

"Yes, yes, he was. But—"

"That's what I thought." Elizabeth raised her cup to her lips and sipped some tea. "The thing is, when I mentioned it to the captain, he told me he was out of town that night. All night."

"Did he really?" Priscilla seemed to be having trouble breathing. "He must have forgotten."

"I don't think so." Elizabeth lowered her cup. "I just can't imagine why he would lie to me."

Priscilla's gaze darted all over the room again. "Perhaps you should ask him, your ladyship."

"I did. He wouldn't answer me. Which is why I'm asking you." She covered one of Priscilla's hands with her own. "Priscilla, Wally is a good friend. If he's in trouble, then I want to help."

"That's very kind of you, your ladyship, but I assure you Wally isn't in any trouble, at least as far as I know. Oh dear." She reached down for her handbag, opened it, drew out a large white handkerchief, and proceeded to blow her nose. "I suppose I'd better tell you the truth," she mumbled as she tucked the handkerchief back in her handbag.

Anticipating the worst, Elizabeth's heart seemed to drop like a stone in a well. "Please do. I'll do all I can to help."

To her surprise, Priscilla actually smiled. "I don't think we'll be needing your help, m'm, except to ask you to keep this to yourself. You see, I was with Wally on Sunday night. We . . . er . . . wanted to be together, you see."

It took a moment for Elizabeth to understand, and it was Priscilla's obviously painful embarrassment that finally made everything clear. "Oh, my goodness."

"I'm sorry, your ladyship, but you did ask. You see, since I share my house with someone, it seemed better if we went to the captain's cottage. I stayed until it was almost light, and then he took me home. So no one would see us together."

"I see," Elizabeth said faintly.

Priscilla drew something on the tablecloth with her finger. "I must ask you, m'm, not to repeat this to anyone. Wally would have kittens if he knew I told you. He's gone to such great pains to keep all this quiet, at least until he's in a position to make an honest woman of me. He always leaves the pub before I do, and last Sunday he waited for me in the lane so's no one would know we were together. That's why he lied. He was protecting my good name."

Elizabeth stared at her for a long moment before saying, "Thank you, Priscilla. I promise I'll keep your secret, of course."

"Thank you, m'm. Wally wouldn't like for it to get out. He's an honorable man."

Elizabeth studied her glowing face and wondered what the fussy little woman would say if she knew just how much she envied her.

Several minutes later she was on her way back to the Manor House. Now, thanks to Priscilla, she knew what it was she'd been missing all along. It was staring her in the face all the time. No wonder she'd had that familiar feeling of knowing something she couldn't remember. Now she had to call Earl—the only person she trusted to help her. And pray that she wasn't too late.

"It doesn't look as if she's going to show." Earl leaned back in his chair and surveyed the crowded lounge bar of the Tudor Arms.

Elizabeth frowned at him. He had chosen a secluded corner table for them, but she still felt as if every eye on the place were on them, watching for the slightest hint of intimacy. "She's not always on time. Alfie said he expected her any minute."

"That was twenty minutes ago." Earl looked at his watch. "We'll give her another ten minutes."

She nodded, and sent another furtive glance at the bar, where American airmen stood shoulder to shoulder with British soldiers and a group of giggling girls in Land Army uniforms. At least they all seemed fairly complacent tonight, which was a relief. Stories about the bar fights in the Tudor Arms were legendary.

Earl leaned in toward her, pitching his voice low enough for only her to hear. "When did you first suspect that Bridget might be the spy?"

"This morning." She sent another glance around her, then reassured, she leaned in as well. "Priscilla told me that she and Wally had gone to great pains to hide their . . . er . . . friendship, but Bridget knew about it. She'd told me two days ago that Wally and Priscilla were close. Priscilla said that Wally took her home early Monday morning. I think Bridget saw them, because she was there at the cottages, paying a visit to Basil Thorncroft."

"She could have noticed the captain paying attention to Priscilla here in the pub. Bartenders have a sixth sense about this stuff."

"I thought of that." Elizabeth picked up her sherry and took a sip from the slender glass. "But that doesn't explain the broken barrel."

Earl shook his head. "You lost me."

"Marlene said that Peter Weston almost ran her over because she'd fallen off her bicycle, thanks to a broken beer barrel in the road. Bridget told me she'd gone into North Horsham to pick up some extra beer because they'd sold so much the night before."

"I still don't get it."

"The coast road is full of bumps and holes. Bridget must have been in an awful hurry to bounce a beer barrel off the lorry."

"That still doesn't mean—"

"Earl." Elizabeth leaned closer. "The coast road doesn't go to North Horsham. It winds around the village and leads out to the American airfields. If Bridget was in a hurry, why did she go so far out of her way that morning? Unless she planned on stopping at Basil Thorncroft's cottage."

Earl pulled a face. "You do have a point. Certainly one worth checking out."

"That's what I thought." Elizabeth leaned back. "All I want to do is ask her a few questions. Which is why I wanted you along, in case I'm right and things get out of hand."

"I still think you should have talked to the constables."

"I don't trust them with this. It's too important. George and Sid do their best, but they've been retired for too long.

They're not only rusty with their skills, they're not capable of handling someone like Bridget."

"They could have called in the Secret Service guys."

"And what if I'm wrong? Think of the trouble it would cause, not only for Bridget, but for Alfie and Ted Wilkins, the owner of the Tudor Arms. I'd never live it down."

Earl grinned. "And we can't have the lady of the manor viewed as a vengeful mercenary."

She pursed her lips. "This is no laughing matter."

He was instantly serious. "You're right. Besides, I heard that intelligence found evidence of someone having spent some time on the top floor of the windmill. If it wasn't the bird-watcher, then it could have been the spy. If you're right about Bridget, though, I'd like to know how she got him to go up there."

"She could have forced him up there somehow." Elizabeth glanced at the counter, where Alfie was frantically trying to keep pace with a rush of orders. "You haven't seen her yet, have you. She's a very sturdy lady."

"She's also more than half an hour late. What do you want to do about it?"

"I'll speak to Alfie." She rose, and Earl scraped back his chair.

"I'm coming, too."

"Thank you." He followed her to the bar, where she edged her way through the crowd to the counter, amid several curious glances.

Alfie caught her eye at once. "I don't know what's happened to Bridget. Maybe I should send someone up there to see if she's all right. I could use her right now. Things are getting busy." He pulled a large white cloth from his shoulder and mopped up a puddle of beer on the counter. "She's never this late as a rule."

"I'll be happy to go up to her room," Elizabeth said quickly. "Which room is it?"

"Number four, but I couldn't let you do that, your ladyship. I'll find someone—"

"Nonsense. You're far too busy. It won't take me a moment." Before he could give her any more argument, she made her way to the door behind the counter with Earl close behind her.

"I've never been back here," she told him as they climbed the narrow, creaking stairway. "It's quite archaic, isn't it."

"This place has to be a hundred years old," Earl said, his voice echoing in the ancient rafters above their heads.

"More like three hundred. Ah, here we are." She paused in front of a dark-stained door with a modern polished brass lock that seemed grossly out of place in the antiquated hallway.

"Let me," Earl said, and stepped forward to rap loudly on the door with his knuckles. After several moments of silence from within, he rapped again and rattled the handle. The door opened and swung into a darkened room. "It's unlocked!" he exclaimed, rather unnecessarily.

Elizabeth hissed out her breath and stepped into the room. The blackout curtains had been drawn, but spilled light from the hall lamps was enough for her to determine that no one was there. She reached for the switch and snapped on the light, blinking at the sudden contrast.

The bed had been neatly made, as if expecting its occupant that night, as usual. In fact, the entire room was neat and tidy, and a quick inspection of the wardrobe and drawers revealed them to be cleared of all belongings.

"She's gone," Elizabeth said on a note of defeat. "We're too late."

Earl had stepped past her and stood by the window,

looking down at something on the other side of the bed. "Wait a minute," he said. "What's this?" He stooped down, then rose with a crumpled paper in his hand. "She must have been in a hurry. Looks like she dropped something."

Elizabeth rounded the bed to join him. "What is it? Anything interesting?"

Earl smoothed out the paper and studied it. "Looks like a flight plan of some kind."

"Oh, dear, that's what I was afraid of." Elizabeth sank onto the edge of the bed. "She must have stolen it from the base. Goodness knows what information she's taking back to Germany . . ." She broke off, then added softly, "No wonder she didn't sound as if she came from Birmingham. I should have realized that."

"What?" Earl glanced at her, then went back to studying the paper in his hand.

"Oh, it's nothing . . ." She paused, watching his face. "What is it?"

"It's this flight plan. It can't be the base . . . and yet it looks . . . holy cow!"

Elizabeth surged to her feet. "What? What is it?"

"It *is* the base. Only not the part we're using. This is the abandoned runway. You remember? I told you we were planning on building a rec hall there."

She stared at him. "Do you think Bridget is planning on flying out from that runway?"

"I'm saying we should get out there and take a look. I'd better put in a call to the base first."

"Come on then!" She rushed out of the room and down the stairs, heedless of the worn carpet snatching at her feet. Earl bounded down behind her, and she waited feverishly in the bar for him while he put in a call to the base.

"They're checking it out," he told her as she climbed into the Jeep. "Though I can't see an enemy plane taking that much risk flying into a military base."

"Neither can I." Elizabeth grabbed her hat as the wind buffeted it. "But what if Bridget plans on stealing a plane and taking off down the abandoned runway?"

"That's a possibility."

Elizabeth winced as they bumped and bounced along the coast road to the base. "Will they shoot her down if she takes off from there?"

"More than likely," Earl said grimly.

Elizabeth was silent for a moment, then said in a small voice, "War is a terrible thing."

In answer, he let go of the wheel and squeezed her hand. The response made her feel much better.

They arrived at the base a short while later, and Earl asked her to wait in the Jeep while he went in and made sure the abandoned runway was being covered before he took her home.

She would much rather have gone in there with him, but had to agree this was not a good time. Instead, she made herself as comfortable as possible on the hard seat.

The combination of the sherry, the excitement, and the blast of wind in her face had taken its toll on her energy. She closed her eyes a moment to rest them, then opened them again when she heard the engine of a vehicle coming up fast behind her.

She turned around, just in time to see a Jeep lurching past her, with a woman hanging grimly on to the wheel. There was no mistaking those hefty shoulders and flaming red hair. It was Bridget, and she was making a clean getaway.

Elizabeth craned her neck, peering through the wire fence that separated her from the building into which Earl

had disappeared. Frantically she looked for the guard, but
he had vanished around the side of the building. By the
time she alerted him and everyone else, Bridget would
have made it to the main road and could take any one of
the crossroads into a maze of winding lanes. She had to
be stopped now.

Trembling with excitement, Elizabeth slid over behind
the wheel. She had watched Earl start up the engine and
it really didn't look too difficult. Turn this switch up here,
step on this clutch thing here, and push down. She tried
it, and nothing happened. Frantically she stomped on it
again, and the engine roared to life.

She shifted her foot to the next pedal, jiggled the gear
lever, and with a nasty grinding noise she was off, ca-
reening from side to side down the road. Obviously there
was a lot more to driving the dratted thing than she'd
realized.

Still, she was moving, and at a pretty fast clip. Bridget,
however, was quite a distance down the road and Elizabeth knew she could not catch up before the other Jeep
reached the main road.

Unless . . . she took the shortcut—a narrow cart path
that soared over a steep grassy hump and across a field.
The path would bring her out onto the road just ahead of
the crossroads.

The opening came up too fast for her to give it any
more thought. She swung the wheel, overshot it, and had
to swerve back to make the opening. She went through it
more or less sideways, and for an awful moment thought
she was going to overturn the Jeep.

It tottered on two wheels for a few yards then, to her
immense relief, righted itself with a sickening thud and
she was off again, soaring and thudding, bouncing and
lurching, until her teeth rattled and she was quite sure

she'd never be able to sit gracefully again. She didn't know how to turn the lights on, and had to rely on memory and the little she could see in the pale glow of the moon. Even so, she kept her foot down on the pedal and prayed she wouldn't hit anything.

It was only then that it occurred to her that even if she managed to halt Bridget's Jeep, she was no match for the brawny woman. She couldn't possibly overpower her single-handedly. What's more, Bridget had probably killed two robust men. She wouldn't think twice about getting rid of a fragile woman.

It was too late to think about that now, however. She'd just have to stop her somehow, and trust to the good Lord to take care of the rest.

The Jeep reached the end of the path and burst out onto the road. Unfortunately, Elizabeth misjudged the steering wheel, and swung just a little too hard. The Jeep skidded in a wide circle, then rose on two wheels. She thought it might right itself, as it had before, but it was not to be. With a shuddering sigh, the Jeep toppled over on its side, sending Elizabeth sprawling headfirst into the wide ditch.

Stunned, she lay there, only half-conscious of the roar of another engine coming upon her at high speed. Then came an ear-splitting screech, a loud crash, and the earth shook. Something rolled noisily across the road and came to rest a few inches from where she lay. Then silence for several seconds, followed by a hum of engines in the distance.

As Elizabeth's head began to clear, she wondered what had happened to Bridget. She rather hoped that the crash she'd heard had stopped the Jeep. At the same time she fervently prayed it hadn't killed the woman. The last thing she wanted was to have someone's death on her conscience. Even if she was the enemy.

Cautiously she moved her arms and legs. Nothing seemed to be broken, though she hurt in some very personal places. She turned her head and listened, but she could hear nothing except the approaching vehicles, getting louder by the minute.

She'd just rest a minute, she told herself, then she'd take a look. Right now it all seemed too much trouble. She closed her eyes, and when she opened them again, she thought she was dreaming.

She wasn't in the ditch anymore. She was lying on soft grass at the side of the road, cradled in two very warm, very cozy arms, while Earl's voice muttered urgently, "Elizabeth? For God's sake, Liz, talk to me. Tell me you're all right."

"I'm all right," she mumbled. "What happened?"

"You crashed the Jeep. God." He gathered her closer, pressing her cheek against the buttons on his uniform. "I thought you were dead. You've gotta stop scaring me like this. You'll make an old man of me."

There was something she needed to know quite badly, but right now she couldn't seem to think of it. All she could think about was that she was lying with her shoulders in Earl's lap. It didn't seem to matter that there were people milling around with someone barking orders at them. She was just too darn comfortable to care.

A warm hand stroked the hair back from her forehead. "Elizabeth?"

She made an effort to rouse herself, and remembered what it was she wanted to know. "Bridget?"

"She's on her way back to the base under guard."

"She's all right?"

"A bit bruised up but she'll live."

"What will happen to her?"

"Prison, I reckon. From the little I could get out of our

guy in intelligence, I found out her real name is Brigitte Wallendorf, and she's on a British government list of suspected spies. They're pretty happy to get their hands on her. She tried to steal a plane, and when that didn't work, she stabbed one of our guys and stole his Jeep."

"Oh, dear. Is he all right?"

"Dead. That bitch is an expert."

"I'm so sorry."

He looked down at her, and in the lights from the vehicles, she could see the anguish ravaging his face. "It's you I'm worried about. I saw you take off after the Jeep, and I remembered you saying you couldn't drive. Then it seemed as if the whole darn base was chasing you, and I was scared they might mistake you for Bridget. It took me a while to find another Jeep to come after you. By that time they'd caught up with you both and were dragging you out of the ditch. The medic said there doesn't seem to be any serious damage but—"

She lifted her hand and placed a finger on his mouth. It was a delightful sensation, and she left it there probably longer than she should have. "I'm all right. Really. I could get up, but I'm just too comfortable to move."

She was pleased to see his face break out in a grin. "That's my girl."

She rather liked the sound of that. His girl. All right, so she had no business being his anything. It didn't seem to matter anymore. His life in America was thousands of miles away in another world, while right then, right there, he was with her, holding her as if he hated to let her go.

Would it really be so awful of her to enjoy these moments, and take what she could from them? Would it be such a sin to love him the way she wanted to love him, as long as she was prepared to let him go when the time came?

Maybe not. Then again, once her head cleared completely and things got back to normal, she might think differently. Only time would tell.

The Homefront Mystery Series

BY M.T. JEFFERSON

IN THE MOOD FOR MURDER

It's murder-by-mail as Kate Fallon tracks a series of letters sealed
with a curse, and tries to catch the killer who's casting a shadow of
suspicion over her hometown...

0-425-17670-3

THE VICTORY DANCE

Kate Fallon's got a beau fighting overseas in World War II,
a crush on Frank Sinatra, and a passion for murder mysteries.
But real-life foul play is about to turn her crime-solving hobby into
a life-threatening dance with death...

0-425-17310-0

Available wherever books are sold
to order call:
1-800-788-6262

(Ad # B456)

KATE KINGSBURY

THE MANOR HOUSE MYSTERY SERIES

In WWII England, the quiet village of Sitting Marsh is faced with food rations and fear for loved ones. But Elizabeth Hartleigh Compton, lady of the Manor House, stubbornly insists that life must go on. Sitting Marsh residents depend on Elizabeth to make sure things go smoothly. Which means everything from sorting out gossip to solving the occasional murder...

A Bicycle Built for Murder
0-425-17856-0

Death Is in the Air
0-425-18094-8

For Whom Death Tolls
0-425-18386-6

Dig Deep For Murder
0-425-18886-0

Available wherever books are sold or to order call
1-800-788-6262

First in the Victorian Mystery series featuring
Dr. Alexandra Gladstone

This country doctor thinks she's seen everything.
Until she finds an earl who's
been murdered—twice.

SYMPTOMS OF DEATH

Paula Paul

0–425–18429–3

When the old country doctor of Newton-upon-Sea
passed away, he left his daughter Alexandra the
secrets of his trade. Now, the village depends on its
lady-doctor Gladstone for its births, deaths, and all
the inconveniences inbetween.

"Don't miss it." —Tony Hillerman

Available wherever books are sold or
to order call 1-800-788-6262

*The National Bestselling Beau Brummell
mystery series*

by
ROSEMARY STEVENS

"Excellent."—*Publishers Weekly*

"Delightful."—Dean James

"Simply Inspired."—*Mystery Reader*

The Tainted Snuff Box   0-425-18441-2

The Bloodied Cravat   0-425-18539-7

Murder in the Pleasure Gardens
                          0-425-19051-X

Death on a Silver Tray   0-425-17946-X

AVAILABLE WHEREVER BOOKS ARE SOLD OR
TO ORDER CALL: 1-800-788-6262

(ad # b467)

LOVE MYSTERY?

From cozy mysteries to procedurals,
we've got it all. Satisfy your cravings with our monthly
newsletters designed and edited specifically for fans of who-
dunits. With two newsletters to choose from, you'll be sure to
get it all. Be sure to check back each month or sign up for
free monthly in-box delivery at

www.penguin.com

Berkley Prime Crime

Berkley publishes the premier writers of mysteries.
Get the latest on your
favorties:
Susan Wittig Albert, Margaret Coel, Earlene
Fowler, Randy Wayne White, Simon Brett, and
many more fresh faces.

Signet

From the Grand Dame of mystery,
Agatha Christie, to debut authors,
Signet mysteries offer something for every reader.

Sign up and sleep with one eye open!

B112